Ocean

Bruce Pascoe was born in Richmond, Victoria in 1947. He has worked as a teacher, farmer, fisherman and barman, but in recent years has been writing and publishing. He and his wife, Lyn Harwood, founded the influential and popular *Australian Short Stories*. He has two children and lives in the Otways, where he is a proud member of the Wathaurong Aboriginal Cooperative.

Other books by the author

Short stories

Night Animals Penguin 1986
Nightjar Seaglass 2000

Novels

Fox McPhee Gribble-Penguin 1988
Ruby-eyed Coucal Magabala 1999
Shark Magabala 2000
Earth Magabala 2001

Non-Fiction

Cape Otway: coast of secrets Pascoe 1998
Wathaurong, too bloody strong ed. Pascoe 1997

Ocean

Bruce Pascoe

First published by Bruce Sims Books, 2002
68 Abbotsford Street, Abbotsford Vic. 3067
brucesims@ozemail.com.au

Copyright © Bruce Pascoe 2002

Cover designed by Stephen Pascoe
Cover painting from 'Musquito' series by Lin Onus: i Tegg's legacy,
1979–82, synthetic polymer paint on canvas, 161 x 74.5cm.
Collection: Aborigines Advancement League, Melbourne.
Reproduced by permisson.
Typeset in Palatino by Midland Typesetters
Printed and bound by McPherson's Printing Group

National Library of Australia
Cataloguing-in-Publication data

Pascoe, Bruce
Ocean

ISBN 0 9577800 6 0

I. Title
A823.3

Distributed by Australian Book Group, 03 5625 4290,
Fax 03 5625 3756

For the Bass Strait women

The author wishes to acknowledge the Literature Board of the Australia Council, the Federal Government's Arts funding organisation, for assistance while writing this book.

Contents

One   Sea Elephant   1
Two   Tamar   63
Three Wybalena   85
Four   Dalrymple   118
Five   Barren   150
Six   Barmah   160
Seven Fair Deal   179

Acknowledgments   191
Families of the Ocean   193
Map   195
Glossary   197

One

SEA ELEPHANT

We arrived at the same time as the Moonbirds. We, with our tall, white sails and they with the shadow of their million wings one flat black sail pressed to the sea. Our first journey this far south and theirs but one breath in the life of galaxies.

That is how we met, the new and the old. Now I'll tell you how we behaved, how we loved, how we killed.

I'm not a man used to writing, so please be patient. In fact, I'm not a man used to exploring the wellsprings of life. But that's what it's come to. I've got the sealer's disease and will die of it before long and I will die alone. Another sealer's disease.

Deal Island in winter is no place for a man to have hope, so I have forsaken that and intend to explain myself to myself, my ship and my maker, whoever the latter may be.

It was me who brought them to Port Phillip, me,

Captain Caleb Mathew and the *Ocean*. I remember Reverend Knopwood very well, I remember how calmly he visited the Great South Land, how he explained away the souls of the natives, the iniquity of the convicts and God's beneficence in having created Port Phillip Bay for the delight of the civilised sensibility.

It was my table, I was the Captain and that's how I came to be there, listening to all this learned talk of state and cloth. I went along with it to be sociable but really I was just waiting for the *Ocean*'s contract of Crown Service to come to an end so I could pursue my fortune in the search for whales and seals, and all that their hides and juices could bring me. See, we were just men, and not very good ones at that and it's men that make history. And women? Well, I never did understand what women were meant to do.

I *can* tell you about men and class and I can assure you that men of my class and background were not meant to become ships' captains, first mate perhaps, bosun often, cook always, but never captain. Except in a time when the Spanish and French carve a wedge through your navy leaving unguarded outposts of the great British Empire in distant corners of the globe, and as a consequence ships all over the place and not enough sober seamen to sail them. So, reluctantly, they make me, Mathew, captain of the *Ocean*.

Oh, I was proud then, don't think I wasn't. Fitting out for the uniform was my ascension to the throne, but I had no one to tell, no one to show off to, just me and the mirror and a fancy man with a tape measure getting impatient with an upstart Irishman.

Look, I'm no good at telling stories, all I can do is tell you about my life and where do you start that? I could say I loved a woman. Two women. I could say I betrayed them both. I could say I killed a man. Several men. I could say I rose from pauper to captain, but I've already said that. I could say I had a mother. And a father. And brothers. But I can't start with them. I can't start with that shame, so I'll start with the other great shame. Does a dying man turn to God? Do his sins become the fuel of fate? Well, I'm trying to explain it to myself and I'm not getting far, so it might be easier to tell someone else. You. Whoever you might be and however you might judge me.

I killed a man. Several men. I know I said that before but it's how I always start when I tell this story to myself. Not with the uniform and the mirror, not with the Captain's table, but with death. And oppression. Theft. All the things an Irishman promises himself he'll never do. Especially for England and especially after what happened to us.

So, the dead.

We were still drawing bits of the coast onto paper. You see a bay, you see a cape, you see a name. Good Hope. Land of Fire. Biscay. But here we thought we were inventing the land. That our pens and sextants were bringing it into being. We had what Bass and Flinders had done, La Perouse and Baudin and the Portuguese, but we were drawing in the gulfs and bays and rivers.

Collins was nothing like Flinders. He hated the place. Couldn't care less about the bays and wooded headlands, he wanted to do the job and get out. That woman was no help. All she could talk about was The Strand, King's Hall, the Palace – as if someone like her would ever curtsy there. She was a whore. Who cares about her body? Bodies are bodies, but she was a whore in her head – and Collins was a bored clerk. Not a seaman's slop bucket.

I was no different. I could see the country and I had parts of it picked out in my head, all I wanted was to be free to take them for myself. Sipping tokay with Knopwood and Collins was a fraud but it wasn't my greatest shame by any means.

So, the dead.

It wasn't all our fault – at first. In the early days, sailors told stories of being offered women and food but suddenly it all changed. You'd come to a bit of coast and expect the same – opportunity, but now they wanted war. We never worried too much about why, we just thought they'd got greedy and ungrateful. And we could understand that. Greed. So we treated them like greedy and treacherous children. And now they were dangerous children.

When we left Collins for the last time his ship, *Calcutta*, was getting ready to sail for Hobart. Our part of the contract was over. There was plenty of good land at Port Phillip and Western Port but Collins didn't want to find it and we didn't want to show him his error. Our fortune was to be made in seal oil, not greasing the palms of government.

We sailed past Western Port and were preparing to begin our catch on the Glennies but some of the men spied a group of natives and sought to make an offer for their women. Such was their haste the longboat over-turned in the surf and they scrambled ashore only to be set upon by the natives. One man went down and appeared dead and the others looked likely to follow, so I had the other boat lowered and we fired our muskets from outside the surf, killing several of the men. I saw my charge catch a young warrior in the side of the head and he fell, mortally wounded, but offered no sound, still attempting to launch spears from where he lay. Our fellows on shore chased and captured a woman and two girls and dragged them into the surf where we soon had them loaded into our boat.

The two girls were beautiful. But men like us, deprived for so long, are unreliable witnesses.

But don't think that's it, there's worse to come, I just wanted to get the tale underway.

We had no idea what we were doing. There were seals enough to keep us employed for several voyages. Our cargo could be sold in Botany Bay, the East Indies or, if need be, in London itself. In our voyages on behalf of Collins and company we'd noted the abundance of seals and whales, and even before setting out for New South Wales we'd heard the drinking brag of sealers returned from Bass Strait.

We'd prepared ourselves as best we could. In our hold we had four try pots, casks for the oil, presses and bales for the skins, building materials and tools, medicines and weapons.

The bountiful seal colony of the Glennies was known to us so, when we arrived, we sailed amongst the group looking for a likely harbour and place for our camp. Flinders had described one of the group as having a fine north-east facing anchorage and that seemed to fit the description of a large curved bay backed by a small creek. We could see a good spring on the flank of the island's peak and it was obvious water would be no problem. I couldn't help thinking of Collins and how he resisted the offerings of the country's embrace.

We anchored in the bay and made ready to make the ship fast for the night before going ashore at dawn. Although we'd seen native canoes in the area earlier in the day there seemed no inhabitants on this island. Just in case, we kept the women below. After dinner I took my wine onto the deck and gazed across at the island and the serenity of its bay softening in the haze of evening. With my telescope I could see seals coming ashore at the northern rock ledge. What a perfect opportunity.

You might wonder at my mild approval of such a remote and wild island, so distant from the spoils of civilisation, but there was nothing left for me in what others liked to call home and most of my crew could never set foot on civilised land except in chains so, for us, this place was good enough. Sea Elephant Bay we called her, after her seals.

I didn't care for the distress in the women's eyes but you have to understand that we meant them no harm. I'd selected my men with an eye to such things, men not so depraved and unreasoned that they would needlessly commit violence. But they needed women and so did I and what women of our own would consider a home perched on the edge of the world's last ocean?

I sipped my wine, smoked the pipe and imagined the little village we'd build here. A couple of huts for the men and myself, a shed for the skins, a cookhouse, and a jetty to the south of the creek. I placed each of these with the mind of an artist, or so I pleased myself to think, and even contemplated a bench at the edge of the sand from which to admire the bay at the fall of evening. This wasn't going to be a hovel of shit and semen and stinking sailors. This would be a little town of honest working men. That was my dream.

I had to dream. Without dream the reality was too stark. I might be captain, but in these latitudes, one hundred and sixty days from London, law and conscience were half-remembered notions. Only clergymen of Knopwood's kind could survive here, only governors of such laxity as Collins could tolerate the crudity of the civilisation. And I knew I was barely in charge of my own ship. While I could supply grog, women and tobacco I would be endured, the promise of the share of the seal bounty was too far off to command the concentration of men whose concentration span was that space of time between ejaculations. They weren't bad men, not as bad as I'd met, but if anyone was to build a bench solely for the pleasure of reverie I'd be doing it myself. I tapped the pipe against the rail and sighed, in no mood to face the eyes of the women or the debauch I could hear beneath the boards of my commission.

The ship's owners had taken on the government contract in order to pay our way to Van Diemen's Land, their profit would come from the seals. The men seemed conscious of this and, next day, set to work removing our stores to the island. By evening we had a village of tents, a try pot rendering the blubber of twenty pup seals and already we could see that a few months would fill our hold with skins and the very highest quality oil.

Of course it didn't stop the men quarreling over women and the performance of the more mundane tasks, but that's what they say isn't it, there's always trouble in Paradise? We brought the seeds for it onto the new land.

That first evening I sat on a cask overlooking the bay and listened once more to the bacchanal in the tents, the men arguing over first use of the women, a greater share of the grog. But at least we were all healthy. I had been scrupulous in that regard and began wondering about the girls and how they might be, these southern savages.

One of the girls tried to swim the passage to the smaller island opposite our camp, but the men took to the boat and the oars as if on a holiday fishing expedition and brought her back to the shore knocked senseless and half drowned.

We had to shackle her by the ankles with insufficient chain to run but just enough so she could open her legs. See, I'm telling everything as it was and you're saying to yourself that a word or two different here and there, a rearrangement in other places could save me from much shame, but there is no saviour from shame while it is in you and you have no God to blame for it.

I'm not afraid of your judgment because that must be measured against our circumstances. And so, my labours by this whale oil lamp are not expiation but explanation. I'm trying to make you understand how it was and how we began our lives in these parallels.

On our first morning ashore the men stood around the women's tent laughing at the dreadful state they were in.

'We poured the rum down the sluts' throats. Now they know the life of a sailor.' Vanderlin was a humorous chap normally, but this wasn't one of his better jests. He came aboard in Copenhagen and we passed him off as an Englishman, Anderson, for the sake of customs. He had been at sea all his life: cooper, sail maker, carpenter, he could do the lot, never a more valuable hand at sea, but in port he became easily bored with the petty tasks of land.

I got on well with him and made much of making

him supervisor of building our first group of huts. He grumbled a while for the sake of it but soon he had a load of lumber shipped from the *Ocean* and the sweet sound of the saw could be heard for the first time on that land.

While the men were productively engaged I visited the women's tent. In a better story you might have expected me to be beaten off by their eyes but, sad to say, I was not. The girl in chains who the men had taken to calling Fanny was quite pretty, even with her scowl and swollen jaw – and shackles.

I had never struck a woman and I wasn't going to start now and tried to impress on them that they would not be hurt by me, in fact could expect rewards. I left them with a portion of salt beef and a kerchief each. These things were received in silence and left where I had put them. Not a cheerful experience for any of us but my own immediate needs had been met and it cemented the pact between the men and myself. Sealers do not salute their captain, they tolerate him – if he's lucky. It was not the ship which bound us together it was our mutual dissolution and the secrets we shared. What was open between us had to be secret in any other society.

It was probably three or four days later that I climbed onto the roof of the first hut. Vanderlin and Briggs had been busy but complaining of headaches and groin soreness. I laughed, to be part of them. See how we were lashed together? And as they smoked we looked out across the bay to where the *Ocean* rode on her chains.

I was struck by a scene as beautiful as any I'd ever seen painted and turned to the men, longing to ask them if they saw it, the beauty of this land. Their normal coarse chatter was restrained in my company but I could sense that my question would arouse their contempt. Briggs farted.

'I've been thinking that we could build a jetty off that point so that we could bring the *Ocean* alongside. Make the loading easier. We could cut timbers off the mainland and bring them across.'

'Big job,' Vanderlin murmured.

'And the women,' Briggs said, 'it'd give them a way on to the ship, they could set it adrift, leave us stranded.'

There was a point to that.

'I was thinking of a store shed at one end – with a lock, so only we could use the jetty. We could store skins and oil while we took a cargo to the Indies. A few men could keep working here and store the produce in the shed.'

'We'd need enough men to scare off the other ships. A full store guarded by a handful of men would be an easy target for the Americans.' Briggs had a brain. They both did. That's why I relied on them. Look what they'd produced in a matter of days. Within a month we'd have a more substantial settlement than Collins had managed in three.

'Perhaps a cannon on that headland. A shot or two should convince any pirates.' I said hopefully.

'Perhaps.'

We were silent as we smoked. They would appreciate the logic of it and their skills would produce it, but true to the new democracy they had to express mild defiance.

La Perouse had mentioned the wreck of a vessel on the eastern corner of the mainland, a substantial Portuguese galleon, heavily provisioned and lying in about a fathom in a snug cove behind the promontory called Greencape. He also wrote of cannons he'd been unable to recover in the time available but a ship with a base camp a mere two day's sail could spend a week in the recovery.

I didn't mention it to the men. I'd keep that for another occasion. A politician's trump card to be played at a crucial time. Perhaps an occasion when the men were bored with seals or restless for new women.

It wasn't just because I was lonely. I'd been lonely or alone most of my life. I knew how to survive it. And it wasn't because I had any higher morals than any of these other men, but I did try to engage the women in conversation.

It was obvious they knew the land backwards. They collected vegetables to roast, eggs to cook and their skills at fishing were extraordinary. Their physical condition was much better than ours despite the rigours and hazards of their new life. Most of the men refused to eat the 'nigger' food even when I collected the vegetables. Cook's men ate the leaves of New Zealand Spinach to ward off scurvy and I tried to encourage my men to do the same, but most considered it primitive poison. Vanderlin ate the eggs and roasted parsnip and none were too proud to refuse the whiting and mullet I netted in the shallows at night.

The women always watched when I fished, as I watched them. They laughed, I could tell, I was nowhere near as adept as they, but I knew they inspected my net when I left it to dry on a bush near their hut. They'd previously constructed their own net from grasses and bark, but mine was just as efficient as theirs and I could tell they offered it some grudging respect.

One night, the girl not in chains, Belle Vanderlin called her, took one end of the net and held it low in the water while I took the shore end. Her wet skin glistened in the slant of the setting sun as she swam with the net. While I lunged awkwardly through the shallows she left hardly a ripple and when the net was ashore it contained a dozen fat sole and enough mullet and whiting to feed the whole camp for two days.

The men watched greedily from their hut. Not greedy for the fish, but greedy for the sea nymph who rose wide-smiled and beautiful from the sea. I too was transfixed. I wanted to say to the men, 'Can you see what this country is like, a country where you can swim in the water at nightfall, where one sweep of the net can harvest you all you can eat, a country where we might have all we want?' And to the women I wanted to say, 'Let me throw off your chains, let us live here like this together.'

The men were gambling and drinking and eating their share of the fish but I took a bottle of Portuguese Rosé to the women's hut and offered to eat with them. They kept their eyes down while preparing their meal, but I sat anyway, pouring four glasses of wine.

Despite the guffaws and gestures of the men I'd been captured by the ease of the evening, the silkiness of the air and my own desire for a companionable evening. I'm not saying I didn't watch every curve of breast and turn of limb, but I wanted to share my meal, the meal we'd caught together.

The women had developed a taste for rum, which they called korraiyn, although they were ambivalent about wine. The sole were delicious as were their roasted turnips and plantain and the wine was good enough to grace any Captain's table.

I asked each of them their name. The woman wouldn't speak, the girls were ready enough, but I couldn't begin to pronounce the names they gave. They rendered my name, Caleb, as Galub and until this day that is what blacks call me – whenever they choose to speak.

The men soon came to make their demands and so I withdrew to my bench and finished the wine, looking out over what I knew was Paradise – had been Paradise and could still be. As I lifted my chin to receive the wine from the glass, my eye swept across the headlands, the horizon, the last pink edge of clouds and felt captured. I toasted the opportunities of the land and the part I might play in it, but the whoops and howls from the tents sounded as the cries from hell itself.

I'm not saying I was any better than them but I thought they were missing the point, missing the real opportunity the land might offer, not just its fat, but its solace.

I felt terrible confusion. The wine was a draught of the land in my throat. Even from a different hemisphere I felt the wine celebrated an unspoiled land. I imagined sharing that wine on this seat with one of the women, imagined her telling me her secrets of the sea, but how could that be in the cycle of bedlam we had established here? I savoured the wine and mused on the possibilities that a man might take, or a life he might create in time to come, a night he might enjoy not torn by the shrieks and caterwauls of debauch. I imagined one man, one woman and a family, it's true, I was already thinking of these primitive women in these terms, because what might they become without their chains – and we without ours.

In looking back, as I do now, in the absence of there being a forward, I may have been too harsh on the perceptions of the men. The life went on at a pace and peacefulness which has to be considered remarkable given all the circumstances and our own collective heritage. Routines were established and although all were dominated by the industry of seal harvesting and the leisure of grog and women, you would have to say that the place was governed by a remarkable harmony. It had very little to do with me. I've pointed out before the tenuous foundations of my authority, but the harmony arose from the very fact that no authority existed. Vanderlin, Briggs, West and Palmer all had rudimentary egalitarian politics. Vanderlin had seen the excessive oppression of the European courts, Briggs and Palmer had seen a similar oppression by the English of their native Ireland and Scotland and West, having been born at sea, was a law unto himself. They were vigilant to ensure that no man was greater than another. Although Vanderlin and Briggs were given responsibilities in the areas of construction and the oil industry, that authority was respected because of their skills, not because of their status.

In the bedlam of the riotous evening it was easy to forget that Sea Elephant Bay was amongst the more lawful ports of the world, given that every port in the world enslaved women.

And it was this routine of industry which gave the island its peace amongst us. At our leisure, some would sing and play the accordion, some would fish, some would sleep in the sand as indolent as any free man might. And these routines were accepted as the rule, and so if I sat on the rocks talking to Belle and Fanny as they fashioned their nets and wooden dishes, absorbing as much of their previous lives as our languages would allow, it was accepted as a free man's whim, not that it didn't attract ridicule, but it was my business and if I chose to act like a fool with women that was accepted as long as I shared the labour which maintained our strange little republic.

I had this sense that it was not us, but the land itself which shaped us in this way. Liberty, Fraternity and Equality are spoken of in every land but it seemed to me it sprang from this land between the fissures of the rock and every time we drank her water we imbibed her soul.

I could never breathe a word of such ideas in this company and it sounded incredibly pompous to me too, but it rose in me as a result of such witness as I'll now describe.

One day I was smoking my pipe on a flat slab of the reef while Fanny fixed both our nets. It must have been some months after our arrival because she was no longer shackled. I had a line in the water, hoping to catch a whiting or a sweep but Fanny shook her head every time I inspected the bait.

'Koorman,' she muttered, and mimed the seal in an

exact evocation and then began to sing, sweeping her hand over the surface of the water and within a minute a seal came to the surface not six feet from where we sat. The animal stared at Fanny and I swear that communication passed between them.

'What did it want?' I asked. 'How did you get it to come?'

'Women business,' she grumbled, 'seal business.'

The older woman, Woonaji, stepped across the rocks towards us and looked first at Fanny and then quickly at me and then to where the seal finally slipped beneath the surface. Woonaji addressed the departing seal in her language and then muttered something to Fanny, whose face set like stone.

Fanny called that seal to her. A useful skill for a sealer's whore, but not a wise thing to show him. There was no immediate shortage of seals but before long we'd be hunting them on the surrounding islands and mainland beaches. Perhaps Woonaji was reluctant to reveal any more magic than they already shared with their captors.

Any whaler or sealer could tell you of places where the animals were all but eliminated. Maybe, despite their dependency on our goodwill, (we all knew stories of the murder of sealers' girls who had proved un-cooperative) Woonaji was conscientiously keeping the spirits of the land hidden from us, unless of course we were doing that for ourselves.

You think this is blather? You discover a new land, you create a new society, and you examine the thoughts which pass through your head under these strangest of all circumstances. We were in a unique place at a unique time, our problem was that we were ordinary men.

I think it was around this time that the *Black Witch* anchored outside the *Ocean* and Captain Saunders and some of his men came aboard.

The men were happy to have new company and news of Hobart and the Colony. Saunders impressed on me the fabulous price of seal skins and oil being fetched in Sydney and Hobart. He hinted that a ship's captain could make a secret dividend there before re-filling the hold and returning to London and the ship's owners, and still with a very good showing for the time at sea.

Vanderlin and Briggs cocked an ear at this conversation and gave me the wink. Our holds were three parts full already. Saunders and the *Black Witch* were on their way to Sydney for that very purpose. I suggested we might join them and retrieve some useful timber and goods from the wreck of the vessel near Greencape. Briggs and Vanderlin were pleased with the arrangement and left us to examine the native women and alcohol being brought over from the *Black Witch* to enhance the festivities at Sea Elephant Bay.

The night was riotous, filled with curses and screams and the women suffered terribly. I had lapsed into the view that our arrangements with the women were cordial, if not mutually agreed, but the crew of the *Black Witch* were true pirates and raped each of the women en masse, including our own and I felt horror at this transgression. Greater depravity I have never seen and as the bedlam of the night progressed it seemed to matter not what sex was set upon or by whom. The care we'd taken with our own health was now useless and once again the powerlessness of my position was never more transparent. The crew of *Black Witch* outnumbered us almost two to one and besides which I couldn't expect my men to turn against those whom they considered their fellow free men.

Our agreement to sell our skins and oil in Sydney was part opportunism, part appeasement. I had to guide a course at not too great a distance from that which my rebel crew had chosen to follow. We'd become pirates and had now to avoid, where possible, any contact with official colonial shipping.

In our passage to Cape Howe we had a charmed voyage and arrived at the location of the wrecked ship and anchored in the secluded bay where we could remain unobserved from the open sea.

It was obvious the Portuguese vessel had been looted above the water line but in all probability goods of value could still be recovered from below. My crew weren't cheered by the prospect for, like most sailors, they preferred being on the water to being in it. But here my knowledge of the women's skills proved useful. They could dive like the seals they sang to and as they'd refused to leave the ship, being terrified of the Ganai people, they were quite relieved to be given a task aboard the *Ocean*.

A party of men from both the *Ocean* and *Black Witch* went fully armed on to the shore, no doubt intent on capturing fresh women.

West was not a shore man and chose to stay aboard and as the tide ebbed we were able to mount part of the stern deck of the galleon and knock out the wooden plugs fixing a small cannon to the gunwale. Belle and Fanny took a rope beneath the barrel and after several attempts we hooked up ropes to a windlass and drew the cannon toward our hull and eventually brought it aboard. West pointed out a case on the seabed and when lashed to a rope it proved to be as we expected, a supply of 6" ball and priming wicks. We would be able to defend Sea Elephant Bay against anything short of a navy as we already had ample powder.

Fanny and Belle continued to recover coins, plate, and even a small chest of gold bars. Briggs and Vanderlin had drawn a plan which would most likely represent the layout of the ship and the location of the Captain's cabin and I directed the search of the women to those parts of the ship which, fortunately, were easily accessible at this stage of advanced tide.

Despite the labours of continuous diving over a

period of several hours the girls showed no sign of exhaustion and brought up items of a value which would most likely equal the returns of our whole sealing season and yet they showed no interest in the goods themselves. The gold and coins they hardly rated a second look while we couldn't take our eyes off the gold even as the women rose black as ebony and as beautiful as sirens from the turquoise water.

The beauty of this bay far exceeded that of our own harbour in the Glennies and once again I lapsed into marvelling at the beauty of this land.

Fanny arrived at the surface once again holding aloft a bottle in either hand and after several dives we had over two dozen terracotta pipes of brandy and bottles of fine Portuguese Rosé. The women showed slightly more interest in these articles but were infatuated by a handful of brass eyelets from the rotted canvas of the galleon's sails. Belle threaded three of them on to the thong she wore about her neck and I was transfixed by the beauty of her glistening form and the sudden glow of happiness as she fixed her necklace and looked up and caught my eye. We rarely saw them smile and the sudden flash of it was blinding to me. I appreciated the significance of the glow of gold but it brought awful memories of my earlier life and the occasion of wealth affected me less these days than the beauty that surrounded us.

I laughed as Woonaji and the two girls examined a meerschaum pipe recovered from the wreck and plugged it with tobacco, sailor fashion, and took turns to light up. I caught a glint of cheeky complicity in Belle's eye.

West and myself were lionised by the men when they returned from the visit ashore but the light went from the eyes of our women as they watched two native women being rowed out to the *Black Witch*.

Woonaji had collected a great pile of oysters and mussels growing from the timbers of the wreck and even speared an octopus but this meal, as delicious as I've ever tasted, and supplemented with the fine

Portuguese wine, did not lighten the mood of the women as they cast their eyes across to the *Black Witch* at any sound that arose there.

The men, except West, didn't eat the women's food but all admired the gold and emptied several pipes of brandy.

I'd sailed the straits of the Moluccas and parts of the East Indies but this bay was as beautiful as any of them. I drew it on to Flinders' chart as best I could and imagined it might be one of the more amendable places for a man to reside, a line of imagination constrained by the muttered comments of the men as they appraised West of the circumstances of the capture of the native women.

As evening settled, the boat was taken from the *Ocean* to the *Black Witch* several times, transporting men to the revels. I watched the eyes of Woonaji and wondered what thoughts slid behind them. Was she in sympathy with her fellow women, even though she seemed to hold the Ganai people in little regard, or did it turn her thoughts to the occasion when she'd been taken from her own people not six months before? Did she dream, behind the expressionless mask of her face, of her country and family? She had never spoken directly to me, or it seemed to any of the men, despite the intimacies we shared with her. I felt no great sorrow for using her like this, it seemed to me inevitable that men of our kind would seek out women of their kind for just this purpose, just one of many of our activities which would be frowned upon by the law of our land should we ever return to it.

These rebel men filling the starlit night with baleful cries of heedless dissipation were further distancing themselves from their homeland's civilisation. The sea was capable of creating that distance simply by being sailed upon, but men, unconstrained by law, did the rest for themselves. Our souls could never rest easily within the domestic rounds of our fellow British subjects, our guts forever churning the salts of our southern excess and leaving the delights of parish pump and passive pew timid in comparison. We had become pirates. We had chosen to become pirates and all who came in contact with us would be daubed by our brush.

The sounds of wailing and revelry from *Black Witch* welled murderously against the wooded hills of the bay and Woonaji spoke briefly to Fanny and Belle who glanced at me in a way which may have suggested an impotent plea, but I shrugged, not out of indifference but from my own impotence.

I can tell you the date of that night, the exact date, because in a small diary I kept separate from my ship's log I wrote this as I drank the Portuguese wine upon the quiet deck of *Ocean*, the *Black Witch* squalling not a league from our bow and the forest of this southern land gone quiet with the disappearance of the sun and the appearance of men who had shown their enormous power.

This is what I wrote that night the 14.3.1804.

82 gold bars, 175lb
188 gold coins
91 silver coins
26 pieces of silver plate
Assorted silverware, goblets, chain, fixtures.

Value: £56,000 gold
      £33,000 coins
      £5,000   sundries

This was a fortune, even when divided by the nine of us on the *Ocean* and the fifteen on *Black Witch*. Saunders had made sure he observed the weighing of all the metal, but sharing the bounty was the price we paid for each other's silence. My share would be nearly £4,000 and with that a man might not become king, but in a new land like this he could purchase property of the kind none of us could have previously imagined. I mused on how I might live my life following the completion of this voyage and while I shared these musings with speculation on the thoughts of the black women, the greater part of my mind was fixed on what I might become with the bounty received from the voyage of the *Ocean*.

Pirates all. Next day I drank tea on board the *Black Witch* and Saunders and I discussed the disposal of our bounty and decided that Sydney would neither be the safest nor most profitable port for a sale such as ours. Kowloon, Java or Shanghai were considered our best and most anonymous markets.

Saunders bought our cargo of skins and oil at a modest price with a portion of his gold and then prepared for a northern journey up the east coast of New South Wales while we set our sails for Sea Elephant Bay to complete our harvest and re-fill our hull for our masters.

The crew of *Ocean* cheered as we came in sight of Sea Elephant Bay. Such a remote location, so unknown to the rest of the world and yet we now considered it home, one of many homes a pirate might have.

Our days were filled with the sounds of our labours as timber was sawn out for the store sheds and cannon fortifications and the industry of rendering seal blubber was marked by the constant chopping of wood for the try pot fires.

West and myself secured the cannon and primed the first charge and looked back from the headland to the beach and our little township by the bay. We saw men sawing in the pit, others hammering shingles onto the store shed roof, some strolling along the beach carrying tools for one or other of the occupations, women gathering shellfish on the reef, smoke rising from the bakery chimney, a scene of peace and production as pleasant as any Brueghel could paint.

We lit the fuse and the blast fired the ball almost a mile out to sea. All the faces on the beach turned to look up at us and there was a great cheer and waving of hats.

We had secured Sea Elephant Bay, it was ours, we had dominion.

Of course others had been there before us. Every time we dug in the sand we turned up native implements and hearth stones and at the east end of the bay there were small stone huts complete with grass baskets, spears, grinding stones and implements. We allocated the huts to the women but they refused to enter, an act we considered disdain for the rough life of the previous occupants but as the months went by I began to puzzle over their reluctance.

Occasionally we saw a native canoe at sea but it always disappeared quickly and although it had been common on our voyages to see women fishing from the canoes some distance from land, these days we never saw women alone and we all knew why. I suppose it was only natural that the original owners of the huts would avoid the place while we remained.

And if they returned when we left for Kowloon what would they do? Destroy all evidence of our habitation, surely. So we began preparations to defend the island, not just from our fellow pirates but also from raids by the native people.

The cannon was only effective against large ships so we fortified the huts with window shutters and let rifle embrasures into the walls. The men we chose to leave behind had been picked mainly for their indolence, because apart from the responsibility to prepare enough skins and oil for our return, the bulk of their time would be theirs to while away as best they could. They had enough food and grog to last them six months and, of course, they had the women.

Our preparations for sail were done in an air of clamour and excitement which belied the fact that many of us now considered our lives to be, in some part at least, separate from the rest of the world.

Talk began to centre on the exotic whores of the east and the saloons where you could get anything, literally anything.

And Kowloon proved that. Minutes after landing I hardly saw the men again. Our cargo was sold to merchants at the wharf where Briggs, Vanderlin and myself were visited by a procession of Chinese, Malay and French traders. We avoided the English.

Our work finished, and arrangements to fix our departure for England made for eight days hence, the men simply vanished. From time to time I would see one or other of them in saloon or street, on the arm of glittering woman or man, as was their want of the moment, and usually under the influence of alcohol or poppy.

The profit from the sale of our seal products and gold was breathtaking. We hadn't realised how much the world had changed in our absence. My early calculations were ridiculously low.

The wharf was crowded with great chests of tea, caissons and balsa caskets of cardamom, cinnamon, masala, paprika, cummin and turmeric. It enveloped you like the fug of opium and men dropped gold bars into the hands of merchants with almost wanton haste. America and Europe couldn't have enough of the East's carpets, courtesans, cane and cocaine. I saw a panda, a tiger and a white fox-like animal all being swapped for ingots, I saw birds and reptiles, furniture and slaves, all falling to the tumbrels of gold.

I climbed the stairs away from the mad commerce and in the space of one hundred steps was offered everything from alcohol, hemp, women, boys, opiates, monkeys, the skulls of dead children, (one trader showing how handy the eye sockets could be), and any kind of carnality you could imagine. I sought refuge in a tea shop where I drank tea and was offered the same things again, but at a more leisurely, seductive pace, finally settling for a girl who appeared no more than nine but was probably fourteen or fifteen.

She was delightful, smelt of flowers and seemed

rather relieved not to be set upon more crudely, or did I indulge my vanity in that regard? Perhaps the East expresses boredom in ways foreign to us. She offered me a poppy pipe which I drew on cautiously, wanting time to consider my position. I was now richer than I had imagined possible and had been able to send a message to the ship's owners in London advising them that I had deposited an exorbitant amount of gold into Lloyd's chancellery in Kowloon. The hysteria of the transactions at the wharf suggested a madness which could turn to gloom and devastation on the instant. I felt our arrival in the port had been well timed even if by accident.

The figures in my head made my brain reel and in that regard the opium was not helping at all and the girl, sensing my detachment took to my clothing once more in a sense of delicate panic. I suspected her masters would be severe if there was any hint of my dissatisfaction but there was no need for that as she was most industrious.

I gave her two gold coins. One I mimed was for her masters and the other she should hide for herself. And hide it she did in a delectably inventive position. I bade her bring me more tea. She offered to prepare a new pipe which I refused and went to stand up but found myself incapable. I lay on the ottoman overcome by the scents rising to the window and the prattle of voices and sedan wheels on the cobbles of the lanes.

Visions swam like oil on water, disappearing and appearing like phantoms. Pandas and tigers leered at me, the teeth of merchants loomed like mahjong tiles, prim English maids were more evanescent than I remembered, Asian girls were clever with their tiny fingers and tongues and a black skinned women swam to me out of the deep, offering crayfish they clenched in their teeth while water cascaded from their hair like the fountains of Venice, and vases of ginger upended their contents into a bath of gorgeous girls and to pluck that ginger with the teeth could yield a most succulent prize.

I awoke to the tiny clatter of crockery to find a

Chinese servant removing the pipe and cups from the table. I checked my money belt and was relieved to find it intact. Most of my money was secured with Lloyds but despite the recent turn of events my normal caution with money remained.

I took from the wallet a letter my sister had sent some months before and, avoiding all those passages referring to our family troubles, turned to a sentence where she advised that Miss Eugenie O'Breheny remembered me and wished me well. She had been a girl at the time of my departure from Ireland and her bond with my sister was the wreckage our two families endured in common.

I tried to tear the veils of opiate from my brain and recall her face but the raven hair, fine nose and broad smile could have belonged to any Irish girl. Oh, but it did make me pine for that life. Yes, for the life in my own country before that time when being in that land had become impossible.

The men staggered aboard in time for our leaving the port, all except McMahon who had last been seen in a most dissolute state with several women and a largish monkey – or so the men claimed. After two days we sailed without him.

The South China Sea managed a raging storm for our departure but she was a good ship, the *Ocean*, and we were never in danger. With nothing much else to do the men set to cleaning and painting the ship's superstructure, giving fastidious attention to brass and timber, loving care for her canvas and rope. This was our home and we loved her. In port all of us were proud to answer enquiries with, 'I am from the *Ocean*.' She was a pretty ship and prettily named.

The Indian Ocean passage greeted us with endless days of sunshine made pleasant with sea breezes and the wind of our progress.

Most of us had mixed feelings about returning to England. Some had the law to occupy their minds, some wives and children they hadn't seen for eighteen months, and some like myself had run from a family shame or dispute and yet others, like West, simply did not like being on land and if they were preferred it without streets. Even in Kowloon he'd made only a brief excursion into the mean lanes and then returned to the ship where he was happy to smoke his pipe and plait Turks' heads and lanyards to fit us for our return journey. He made a rope mat for the helmsman's feet and it was a work of art. He rowed from ship to ship yarning with the sailors of whatever nationality, admiring their craft and seamanship and learning what he could. The helm mat incorporated the designs Chinese painted on any temple wall not covered in dragons and idyllic rural scenes.

He was good to have on any ship, West, even better for the fact that he hardly spoke. On matters of navigation, sail setting and general seamanship I'd outline my plans in his company and watch the light of his eyes. A nod or grunt would be approbation, a sniff or raised eyebrow and I'd take another sextant reading, drop the lead, or observe the clouds through the telescope until I'd satisfied his instincts. I prided myself not so much on my seamanship, which wasn't scanty, but on my ability to observe those for whom the skin trembled to the ocean currents and the nostrils smelt storms. West was a seaman.

Unhurried by the pleasant and leisurely progress I ruminated on my memories of Eugenie O'Breheny and the preparedness she might have to leave her native land. Well, like me, she'd already left her native land and was living in Wales, only a short passage from Ireland, but a much greater distance of shame.

The memories and uncertainties became the more keen as we left the coast of Africa and sailed the Portuguese coast, rounded Brest and entered the sullen flow of the Thames. Eugenie O'Breheny would have to wait while the ship's company met our masters.

I expected them at the wharf or, at the very least, at the Customs House, but we had concluded our preliminaries before a message came to meet the Chairman at the Imperial Hotel on The Strand.

Sir Wallace Gilbey was a quiet accumulator of wealth but his appearance on this occasion was most unlike his usual gruff impatience. He appeared distracted, almost deferring to my advice on most matters of our commerce.

And the reason soon became clear. He himself was ill and the partnership had suffered some personal and fiscal ructions despite the buoyant nature of London's markets.

For my share of the sale of our cargo they wanted me to take two-thirds in kind. The *Ocean*. Blood bolted in my veins, but I sensed an air of panic in Gilbey which aroused my instinct and I bargained that down to half my share, the ship and new provisions. He was happy to accede because anyone knew that after so long at sea a half share of my cargo allowance was not a great recompense. But I already had the security of gold in the bank – and now I had my own ship. Not bad for an Irishman in exile.

It wasn't necessarily the most risk-free deal a person could make, because ships can sink, but I'd seen Kowloon and even if the rewards were only half as good on our next visit, the ship would be a wonderful investment.

But in accepting the ship so readily I had made certain of my return to Australia, unfettered by the commercial whims of owners who might see more value in the American or African trade.

Gilbey signed over the ship to me, wrote out a bank order for the balance, shook hands, declined to finish his tea and hustled from the room like a man escaping from the brink. Despite the boom in trade Gilbey had come to the edge of bankruptcy and as I finished my tea and rum cake I plotted a brief financial map, spreading my now substantial resources in a number of areas.

Immersed in these deliberations, the preparations for my new life, I looked up and for some time stared without seeing what was before me, until the strangeness became apparent. My fellow diners were as unlike me as a fish is to a flute. While I had scarcely considered what to wear, besides appearing presentable, and that was helped by my captain's uniform, these people had planned their dress and entertainment more completely than they'd prepare for their mother's funeral. The room was aswarm with expensive fabrics cut to a maddening refinement and the voices too were tuned to an excruciating pitch outside the boundaries of kindness and courtesy. I closed my notebook, capped my pen, watched and listened a while before rising and leaving the room to prepare for a short voyage to Wales. I drew up a message for the crew to indicate my return a month hence and fixed it to the shipping notices outside the Ball and Anchor and in the window there I spied the doleful face of West staring out to the harbour. I followed the line of his gaze, knowing as I did it would lead to the *Ocean* riding gently on her hawser.

I entered the hotel and appraised West of my intentions, his eyes meeting mine with little enthusiasm. But then I advised of my eventual plan to begin a return voyage to Sea Elephant Bay within a month and a quick gleam brightened the corner of his eye for a second and he took sufficient heart to accept my offer of another porter. I heard a low murmur.

'Pardon, Mr West?'

'With a dash of rum.'

'Oh, of course, porter with a dash of rum.' He nodded and I felt our verbal correspondence had advanced more in that conversation than for all the previous eighteen months of his service.

I'm sure if I said I was setting sail in a month for Riga, Rio de Janeiro, Maine, Newfoundland or Ceylon it would have been all the same to him. Without saying another word he agreed to get the crew ready to sail by that date and provide himself as first mate for the short journey to Wales. The *Ocean* was ours, or mine at any rate, and we could take her where we would.

As we passed the Eddystone rock off the coast of Plymouth, West took leave of the helm and came to me on the quarterdeck and pointed at the mean fist of sloping rock.

'They're puttin' a lighthouse there. Whale oil light.'

'Really,' I replied, amazed at how far our relationship had advanced.

'They'll be the way of the sea in time. Like the Glennies and the Promontory in Bass's Strait. Lights on all of 'em.' He nodded and went back to the wheel, leaving me dumbfounded by the slow hearts of some wise men. But I had my own slow heart to contend with as we rounded Landsend and made for the port of Milford Haven. What I knew was that you could fall in love, I'd seen men do it, but if it lasted a season it'd be a miracle.

I had in mind an idea to spend my life with a woman, but not a woman who'd get the vapours at first sight of snakes, sharks or rough huts. Perhaps an Irish exile living in the teeth of the Skomer Island gales may have learnt what to expect in rough anchorages and what to expect of the men who visited them. No fine clothes, no fine company, no fine house, but steady labour and the independence to be free of any yoke of blame or torment.

I left West at Haverford handily seated at the hotel window within sight of the *Ocean* and took the ship's boat out to Skomer Island, one of the bleakest islands ever inhabited by men or puffins. The birds love a steep-cliffed island addressed by hurricanes and spume and here they were right at home. The hard grassed paddocks were interrupted by ancient stone buildings and pigsties erected by people who were innocent of saws, drills and mortar. The rock was hewn as neatly as a stone axe could manage, leaving plenty of room for the entry of gales to fiddle with stove and candle.

The present occupants had made desultory use of stucco and shingle, but the rude shapes of the prehistoric houses remained the same. These could only be the houses of those who had shunned all society, or had been shunned by it, and of these Eugenie O'Breheny was the latter.

She was working as a schoolmistress for two or three families of blunt-faced children whose expression most closely resembled soap, coarse, lardy soap. Eugenie had been advised of the day of my planned arrival but not the time, so I wasn't surprised to find her out of the house for, had I been her, you would not have found me in that low kitchen with its smudge lights and steaming offal. I'd seen may things cooked at sea and eaten most of them but knew I would not be eating in this house this evening.

The O'Brehenys, although not wealthy people, had owned land and been used to a style of life far beyond that of the huts of Skomer. I knew I was about to offer Eugenie O'Breheny a proposition which, while not irresistible, presented an unusually attractive opportunity for one in such conditions.

She was sitting against the ruined wall of a stone age hut where it afforded some protection from the wind and snared what there was of the sun, but so pale it failed to bring light to her cheek. She looked out over a sharp-cliffed bay cuffed by a pebbly beach where puffins teemed on the shore and gulls planed at the lip of the cliff, catching the edge of the iron wind.

She rose quietly to meet me, not with the joy of a prisoner about to be freed, but with the resignation of one who might gain a limited freedom, a fragment of joy as large as a family like hers could expect.

'Captain Mathew.'

'Miss O'Breheny. May I sit with you a while?'

She nodded and we sat against the wall regarding the vicious capping of the waves and the mad plunges and shrieks of the wind-torn gulls.

Ocean

'Your journey from Australia was pleasant, I hope.'

'Yes, we had very good fortune.' I looked at strands of hair being whipped about her face and wondered if she had much appreciation of where this place called Australia was located. It was neither a beautiful nor plain face. It was a face of even proportions set with the determination of those who endure adversity.

Our silence lasted several minutes as I watched her. Why should a man and woman have to rely forever on the words spoken in the space of a few seconds? I took an unconsciously deeper breath and she turned her eyes to me, and while you could not describe her look as defiance, perhaps it would be best to say that here was a woman who could account for herself – a quality much required in Australia.

'Miss O'Breheny, our families have suffered greatly in the past decade and both of us have had to flee the home of our birth. I have found my reprieve on the world's oceans and have lately been involved in a most profitable trade, whereas I can see from your current habitation that things are difficult for you. Miss O'Breheny, I own the ship, *Ocean*, and have more than enough money to buy a substantial property in Australia and prospects of much further success in the seal industry. We are of similar age and background and both yet to marry. I wish to ask for your hand in marriage but advise that I intend to live in Australia where the life is hard, although not so hard in comparison to this.' And I waved my arm to indicate gale, broken wall and crude village of stone and poverty. 'I cannot promise a sparkling social life or the comforts of the grand homes – but the great attraction there for me, and perhaps yourself, is freedom from all that has oppressed our families and all the families who live in this tumble of stone. Our children, should we have them, will not grow up as beasts of the cave . . . and I make this further promise, Miss O'Breheny, I will never raise a hand against you and will treat you as well as a man of my social graces might manage, for it is obvious to me that

30

you have an independent intellect and a determination which requires respect – and affection.'

She regarded me with the composure of a woman who had anticipated my stiff speech.

'Captain Mathews, you have not changed since you were ten. As I have not. What we saw then has shaped us both for life and you must forgive me if I say that the opportunity you offer can only be an improvement on what you have witnessed at this place. If you allow that my acceptance is based on the knowledge that I saw, in your youth, a steadiness and honesty I admired and that in my present circumstances I am influenced more by escape than promises of wealth and happiness, I will do my best to provide you with the companion you seem to want. Perhaps we might learn to live in close amity.'

The angels did not sing, cherubs did not blow their trumpets of joy, hats were not thrown in the air or champagne corks explode, but neither of us, it seems, had expected anything of the like.

'But, Mr Mathews, there is one condition I must make. If you would kindly delay your return for fifteen minutes I would like to advise my employers of my resignation for I intend to return with you to Haverford. We will have to find a minister to marry us immediately, which should not cause great difficulty, as neither of us can call on any family who might attend, be it tomorrow or a fortnight hence.'

'Very well,' I agreed and we entered the low hut where she ducked behind a hessian curtain, leaving me with the family who turned from their plates and regarded me, jaws clumping.

'So where's Australia, then?' the head of the house asked at last.

'In the southern hemisphere, sir.'

'Further than Spain?'

'Yes, much further.'

'Do Africans live there?'

'No.'

'Why not?'

'Australia is on the other side of the world and at the other end.'

'Oh,' he said and turned back to his plate, but of course what could he have said to my answer when he was battling to comprehend how the sea managed not to spill out of a land that was supposed to be upside down.

'Got mutton there?'

'Yes.'

'Women?'

'Yes.'

'Does the sun ever set?'

'Yes.'

'How long does it take to get there?'

'One hundred and thirty days.'

'And it's underneath us?'

'Yes.'

Several of the older children looked down at the floor, musing, no doubt, on the whereabouts of a reversed continent, their mother occupied by plunging a ladle in a dreadful pot.

A glance from Eugenie and we left the hut without further comment between any of us, the man, grappling with an improbable concept, his wife still annoying a part boiled sheep's stomach, and the children more aware of the limits to their world.

It wasn't a difficult trip back to Haverford. The sea was a little lumpy and crests were occasionally snatched from the top of a wave and dashed across our bow, nothing unusual about that, but I was interested in Eugenie's reactions. There were none. She neither looked out at the waves with dread or delight, she simply endured.

I was satisfied rather than exhilarated, but in the case of marriage I'd seen little exhilaration. Satisfaction and reliability seemed much more useful shoes for life.

In the midst of preparing the *Ocean* for our return

to London we managed to find a minister who for the sight of a little gold would marry us in the sight of his Lord.

We were strangers to him and him to us but it didn't prevent a standard exposition on our worthiness and undoubted happiness in each other. The form of marriage service having been seen to, the minister shepherded us to the door and perhaps to appear not too abrupt called after us.

'And where do you plan to live, Captain?'

'Australia.'

'Oh, really, is it far?'

'It's a British Colony, your worship, but on the other side of the world.'

'Well, of course, I've heard people say it's a long way. And full of criminals.'

'Not quite full.'

'Well . . . may God be with you then.'

West who was our witness and only guest had been required to say only two words, but whether in our defence or approbation it is hard to say as his sea beard made both incomprehensible. He muttered to himself on leaving, something to the effect that God was unlikely to be found any further than a priest could walk in soft-soled shoes and I began to like West a great deal more.

We barely had enough crew to sail the ship, so for the passage to London I spent most of my time at the wheel and hardly saw Eugenie at all. Not that I hadn't thought of her and wondered how two quiet beasts as we might consummate our physical marriage. But there was no time for too much introspection as I had to both keep to the wheel and hold lanyards while the men fought the sheets. We reefed canvas progressively as a wind had got up from the east and was threatening to dismast us, but once we were at half sail I allowed myself a moment to wonder about her body in the full realisation I had never slept with a woman who hadn't been paid for the service or stolen for the purpose.

The language arts of seduction had never passed

my lips, never been required. This thought was slightly disturbing because I had deliberately chosen a wife at a time when I'd almost given up consideration of marriage and yet it was my determination to treat her well, indeed I wanted to make her happy.

I became aware that I must have taken to nodding my head while engrossed in this thought, because West was regarding me curiously. I feigned a cough and wiped my mouth with my handkerchief while vigorously clearing my throat but I'd have to do better than that to fool West.

Back in port, the loading proceeded in the frenzy of handcarts, wagons, barking dogs and small boys begging to stowaway. We were provisioning for an extended period and there was a constant coming and going of chandlers and merchants and sailors wanting news of the world and the new ownership of the *Ocean*. Our success in the sealing industry seemed common knowledge, no doubt a result of many a brag in any house visited by the *Ocean*'s crew.

I was glad to see the final stages of loading near completion.

After dinner, two nights before our departure, I visited Eugenie in her cabin as no arrangements had yet been completed to fit a double bed in mine.

'May I visit you tonight?' I asked, completing the phrase I'd worked on for five days.

'Of course, you are my husband.'

'I'm sorry about this chaos but once at sea it will be more quiet, we'll have more time to discuss how we are to live.'

'And where.'

'Yes, yes, of course, I've told you very little of any of this. There is a bay, Eugenie, on the other side of the world, which we've called Sea Elephant Bay and it is the prettiest harbour anywhere. Bass's Strait can be wild of course, but on a pleasant day it is one of the most beautiful places I've ever seen, and either there or on one of the other islands I've a mind to settle. I hope you'll be happy there, Eugenie. I know the sacrifice you're making in leaving your homeland with a man you hardly know.'

'I know you, Caleb, we were children together, remember. I know what you're like.'

'Well I hope you can be happy with me then . . . my dear . . . and after my watch I'll visit you . . . if I may.'

After closing the door I stood by the deck rail and wondered about the expression on her face. Was she still sitting by her writing table? Was her face set like stone? Was it lit by a little anticipation? Was her face held in her hands? Or did it mean nothing to her? I wanted her to enjoy our lives together, I didn't want to treat her like a brute as I'd seen many men treat their wives.

Now, as I sit before this page staring out across Bass's Strait it occurs to me that in that night lay the seed of much that was to follow. Whores are paid to show enthusiasm, they are paid to show you their bodies, they are paid to give you pleasure. Eugenie did none of this. Not that she was cold or unkind but clearly she, like I, knew little of the language of seduction, but she, unlike I, knew nothing about the pleasures of the body.

She did not show me her body, perhaps it had never occurred to her that the act of revelation was the basis of physical love, and her ignorance of her own body, and of course mine, made it a difficult, troubling performance. I watch the capping waves and still, thirty-five years later, remember with a flush of embarrassment and anguish the bumping and fumbling, the dreadful silence, two mute bears wrestling as kindly as it is possible for bears to wrestle in the dark. My anguish was not just for myself, but for her . . . what would it be, humiliation? Distress? As I said, much of what was to follow was prophesied in a cabin of the *Ocean* on that grim night on the Thames.

At Cape Town we took on the fresh fruit and vegetables and barrels of lime juice Cook had taught us to consume during the longer voyages. Some crews objected, addicted as the sailors had become to the salt pork and rum on which many captains still considered the common sailor could survive.

My men were marginally more sober and restrained than most, although it would be hard to tell if you saw them at their first port after an extended sea leg.

Eugenie and I stood at the rail watching the chaotic commerce of the port, the coal black vendors, the imperious Dutch planters, the Arab merchants trying to sell everything from parrots in cages to monkeys and exotic medicines. The Africans were a surge of colour adorning the shiny ebony of their spectacular bodies while the Dutch favoured the cool colonial white, contrasting with the flowing striped caftans of the Islamics.

Eugenie watched it all, occasionally asking a question or two about the activity below us but in general just watching the milling and shouting of the masses.

'Look,' I said to her, pointing out a silent man at the back of the crowd sitting on a stack of rattan furniture. 'What do you think, Eugenie, a first purchase for our home?' I set off down the gangway, pushed my way through the crowd and pointed at items of the furniture which I thought might be useful. As I pointed at each, Eugenie would nod. After I had selected what I thought sufficient to furnish a house I pointed at a few improbable items just to see if she would nod her head, and she did. I turned and saw a man offering a monkey on a chain. I pointed at the animal. Eugenie didn't nod but neither did she shake her head. Neither of us wanted a monkey but I wondered whether Eugenie was unsure of her role as wife. I bought a dozen ostrich feathers and a roll of jade silk as a present, trying to find items which would change her expression from quiet acceptance and polite gratitude. Neither succeeded as I felt in my bones it would not.

I returned to the tasks of monitoring the stowage of supplies including the furniture and cloth. West was quietly helpful as usual while Vanderlin, Briggs and Armstrong took leave to satisfy their final lusts before the journey through the Indian and Southern oceans where albatross and seal would be our only warm-blooded companions.

Prostitutes and opium were available in ample and exotic supply even in this remote southern port. They followed sailors as albatross followed ships. If we managed to sail to the moon, we would be met by these women whenever we chanced to dock, some grubby pimp plugging a hooker, smiling with broken teeth, and a woman smoothing a mattress and smelling of flowers.

Eugenie seemed fascinated by it all but it was hard to read what she made of it. Whatever she thought, this would possibly be the last she ever saw of this kind of life, for now we were set to embark on a voyage of ninety-nine days through a stretch of ocean unbroken by any land and attended only by whales and sea birds and later still by masses of floating ice. What would her quiet scrutiny make of that after three months of nothing else?

I hoped she could accommodate the journey and the arrival into the acceptance of the crude life we were about to lead. The visions of boiling try pots, the stench of hot oil, and the profanity and debauchery of the men on land were suddenly made gruesomely vivid, seeing it from the perspective of someone who'd never seen or imagined the life we led in the south.

Whenever I mentioned our new home I drew pictures of remote, pristine bays with mild weather and unlimited peace, but clearly all of those things would be but the backdrop for a smaller version of the chaos and decadence of Cape Town. If we could take prostitutes and opium to the moon we could certainly take them to Sea Elephant Bay.

What would she make of that life? What would she make of me? But though I wished for her comfort and happiness, I'd already decided that this was the life I would follow and if she couldn't tolerate it, well ... well, I hadn't even considered what would become of her if she couldn't tolerate a life somewhat less crude than that she'd left on Skomer, and on a continent, in fact islands off a continent, which the world hardly knew existed.

There was a pang of guilt and trepidation for her future life but it wasn't much more than that. I saw myself as morally superior to the crew and expected that to be sufficient to gain the confidence of any sensible woman, but if it didn't provide a satisfying life well it would be too bad, because now that we were setting our sails for the Great South Land there was no turning back. This was the life we'd lead, like it or lump it.

I visited Eugenie in her cabin periodically for, without a word having been spoken, plans for her to move into my cabin had been forgotten. The arrangement suited me, her silence and constrained politeness got on my nerves and I had very little idea how I affected her. Our unions were of the same order as before although, gradually, we became more adept together and there was less collision and a little more collusion but, once again, what she made of this conjunction I had no idea. I wanted to speak with her about it but could not. I wanted to hint at the delights of African depravity, the lavish skills of those tall black women and the more subtle, if silent, feints of the Palewa women of Bass Strait.

But I didn't have the words for a conversation of that nature. We seemed to walk on eggshells as it was, to make even the most subtle suggestions of more amorous physicality might turn those eggs into shards of glass.

Well, that's what I thought then, but from the vantage of thirty-five years removed I would have to say that I simply did not care to spend the time required to produce a trust between us where such things could be said. I'd had no experience of relationships of this kind, I hardly knew my parents as people and my patience was no match for a task requiring the necessary dedication. I was captain of a ship, after all, and we were embarking on the world's most treacherous ocean crossing, a new sailing route which had already claimed hundreds of lives.

So, while I might have the necessary good will, I had neither the tact nor the time to spare on a task which might not succeed no matter how much was invested in it.

As I said, the seeds for the future had been sown on our first night together but who could you condemn as the planter most responsible? Even now, in more amiable hindsight, I cannot say. Perhaps we were just in the garden together and that in itself was sufficient.

Amongst the ice at last. One dawn, I climbed to the deck to the most eerie silence and a peculiar light which I thought was the portent of a giant storm, but West, at the wheel, angled his head to the right and I looked in that direction and stepped back involuntarily. We were sailing beneath a massive green wall of ice, glowing with a depth of colour you might imagine tinting the halls of heaven . . . or perhaps the rooms of hell. It was a colour which almost had its own noise. Not a hum or a murmur, but a sort of quiring like an over-keyed piano wire. The ice certainly groaned and occasionally alarmed with thunderous cracks.

I turned to order West to stand off into the wind, but I could see he was keeping us out of the shadow of the iceberg's dreadful calm. We were sailing across a bay in the wall which had to be at least twenty miles wide, so wide it seemed to us the size of Wales.

West pointed at a ledge in the ice where some object

hung, flaring white against the deep jade of the ice. I took the glass and brought it in to view, a fragment, maybe ten yards of sailcloth and a league of manila rope snagged on a thorn of ice.

'Canvas,' I said to West and lowered the glass and looked at him. We said nothing as we sailed past and brought it to no one else's attention for to dwell on the fate of the people embayed in that windless shelter would do no one any good. I entered the fact in the log and left it to others to determine which ship's crew and passengers spent their last days, perhaps weeks, slowly consuming all their food while they tried in vain to leave the sucking current of the ice island, breaking body and spirit in search of the wind. The silence of the snag where the canvas hung was possibly no greater than when the ship was still afloat and all hands stared out to an ocean so vast and yet so removed from where they floated, their hull licked and sucked by a giant green beast which would not let them be.

But they had certainty, I was sailing toward confusion.

Even now I cannot tell you what kind of man I was, or am. I had opinions about my independence and passive good will, still do I suppose, but how much of that is the ego quelling the fact.

I sailed toward confusion, leaning at the rail, convincing myself that I had Eugenie's best interests at heart, those of my sailors and those who I'd left behind to guard Sea Elephant Bay. But do any of us act outside greed and self interest?

That voyage north was marked by these thoughts, interrupted by breaching whales and dolorous albatross and ever and ever the great green southerly swells bearing us on.

Readers, there are some of you who hate this maundering introspection, but don't think I'm not one of you, all my life I've leant toward the pragmatic, the worldly, but on that voyage I began to doubt myself and all others. Not my ability, and not theirs, but what we thought we were doing to fill in our years. I had no faith in spirit, no belief in another place and yet all we did on earth seemed so random, so self interested. I stared at men to try and fathom their leagues but they began to avoid my gaze, I pondered the nature of sex, of women, I wondered what made West so satisfied in his gloom, not satisfied perhaps, but so unhurriedly and fearlessly accepting of himself and his circumstance. Anything could happen and he would be ready to do what he could to survive it whereas when I looked at Eugenie I could see her gaze was different, she was conjuring, defying fate, she was going to intercept chance. Perhaps the flight from Skomer was her first interception.

That's the kind of jumble that sloughed inside my head.

I was so unused to this fog that I sought to enquire of Eugenie, to test this state of mind against her opinion.

Gavez, our cook and steward, was a fine acquisition. We'd had him on board *Ocean* several times and we always sought him out whenever we began a voyage. Sometimes other ships had snared him, sometimes we were lucky and ensured our luck by paying him well and treating him to his pleasure. The opiate. Albatross eyes. That's what it was, he had the face of an albatross, away with the waves. But the man could cook and always had us supplied with casks of the best Portuguese wine which we bought for a song.

As Eugenie and I sat back from our plates of mackerel he served us verdhelo from the chilled stone bottles he favoured. The wine was green like the skin of a lime and could bring a sigh of pleasure from the crudest palate. Even Eugenie, who was quite abstemious, would take the glass from her lip with a tiny upward inflection of the wrist in appreciation of the tart limey wine. It seemed like a good time.

'I've been thinking, Eugenie.'

'You always did.'

She remembers me as a boy and seemed to have this idea of me as some kind of dreamer, whereas, as I said before, I thought of myself as the most practical man.

'Oh, it's just that the ship sails herself in these latitudes. You stand at the wheel and your thoughts drift. I've been thinking of our house.'

'Yes.'

'Well the island is so small, it's just occurred to me that you might not like it. It's so remote.'

'I lived on Skomer.'

'Yes, but I would like you to be happy, it's not just furniture and a house, I'd like you to be happy there. It's alright for me, I'm used to that life, I've chosen it, whereas . . .'

'I chose to come with you.'

'But . . . but Eugenie, I want . . .' and I had to almost whisper because men were coming and going as the watch changed. 'I never wanted . . . to insult you with my needs.'

'It is no insult, Caleb.'

'But I didn't want to cause you . . . hurt . . . or surprise . . .'

'I'm not surprised . . . or hurt.'

'I want you to be happy, Eugenie, as happy as me.'

'It is early, Caleb, and neither of us, it seems to me, would be seen by others as happy. Have a look around, Caleb, we are as strange to these others as if we'd risen from the sea.'

'Even West? Gavez?'

She indicated Gavez with a lift of her eyebrow, 'Is that happiness, or disappearance? And West, well, who would know.'

'But . . .'

'And as for happiness, Caleb, it would be unwise to hope for too much. I trust you, Caleb, not to the last ounce of my being, but I trust that you have the interests of others at heart as well as your own. From my experience that is goodness. As for happiness, I have no experience. I will try to reward you for your goodness and generosity.'

Reward. I hadn't been after a reward, I'd been looking for reassurance I suppose, but the conversation seemed finished. She still sat and sipped the wine, still with savour, but there seemed no way of developing our thoughts. I watched the lantern swing and swing with the labour of our progress and hardly saw Gavez replace the bottle with another.

It was never with either relief or joy that we saw King Island. You hoped to see it to confirm that you had made the right approach to the strait, for not to see it could mean you were too far west, fog or storm could mean you were upon it. So it was not joy, not even relief, just a grim acknowledgement. 'There it is, the bastard rock.' King was mean, surrounded by snarling reefs and the most horrible seas you could ever meet. I looked at West and he just stared at the island as you would at a snake that hadn't thought to bite you, this time.

We could all name the ships who hadn't made the passage. *Cataraqui, Surprise, Kalaphone, Europa, Whistler, British Admiral, Brahmin, Arrow, Waterwitch, Blencathra, Netherby*, we knew them all, even the wreckage of ships which had occurred before Black and Flinders had first sailed the Strait. And each of us could recite the stories of those ships and I thought it might be of interest to Eugenie, but wondered if the fate of the women and children clinging to the bow of the *Cataraqui* and waiting to be washed into the sea and death while only two hundred yards from shore might be too bleak even for my wife's sober nature, or perhaps it was myself, couldn't bring myself to name the fear each of us held as we passed that treacherous rock.

Fortunately the weather was mild that week of autumn although the swells which had followed us up from the Antarctic sharpened their peaks in the strait and whereas before we'd been rolled on their fat backs, now we were being punched and slapped by a steeper, more fractious sea. Nevertheless the weather continued mild so by the time we had gained the sanctuary of the Kent Islands we were sailing in a more benevolent sea.

I drew breath as we approached the island from which I had drawn a fortune and now intended to make a home. The tufted brow of Sea Elephant began to separate into the individual trunks and crowns of eucalypt, wattle and tea-tree and I searched it with the glass for the first sign of life; smoke, dinghy, the casual wave of an arm, but as the *Ocean* bore me ever closer down the tunnel of the telescope an uneasiness pressed its thumb to my heart.

The others waited expectantly for me to announce the sight of our fellows but gradually they sensed my apprehension. We rounded the southern point where the cannon was clearly visible but nobody was on the jetty to welcome us, no smoke rose from any chimney, no women gathered shellfish, nothing, the place seemed deserted and I dropped the glass, turned to the men and Eugenie, but all could see for themselves that our island was abandoned.

The boats were gone, even the little whaleboat we took to the outer islands for seals. The men were certainly gone, the women too, no weapon spared, no grog, not a stick of tobacco, not a knife or axe or hat, yet all else remained.

It could have been pirates of course, but then West and I came to the old black camps at the northern end of the island and saw immediately that the houses had new turf on their roofs, flour bags by the fire and warm tea in our own billies. The people had only just left. The blacks. They'd seen our sails and must have been well prepared to leave at a moment's notice.

Not so well prepared, however, that woven grass mats had not been left on the beach and the wood and bark dolls of children left scattered where they had played while their mothers fished. And we looked at the little rocky channel beside the beach and could see the whiting leaping and moiling against the weir made from grass and tea-tree stakes.

West waded into the shallows of the bay and picked up a section of oar blade and stuck it upright in the sand without comment. One of the fleeing craft had met with some difficulty.

On our return to the village, for that's how we'd come to call it, the men were preparing the *Ocean* for passage. My ship. They looked at me and Vanderlin left their ranks and met me before I reached the jetty.

'They've taken everything but the money. Axes, grog, knives, but not the money, left the charts and books, never touched the oil. Niggers done this. We're going across to the mainland to fetch them back. You can come if you wish.' This was effective mutiny. There was no chance of my going with them. How could I take Eugenie, knowing she would witness the purpose of that voyage. I had been made impotent by her presence.

'We'll look after your ship, she'll come back unharmed, but we're going to save our mates, if it's not already too late. West, are you coming?' West looked out at the ship and the sea and shook his head slowly. Never said a word.

Well that was that. We waited uneasily for them at Sea Elephant Bay. I walked up to Cannon Point every few hours to check for returning sails while West took walks along the beach. Eugenie collected the wooden dolls of the black children and spent hours inspecting the stone and turf houses on the grassy verge of the northern bay.

You will probably know as much about that voyage as I do. The fact that you've found this log means that in all probability you've come to it via the Governor's report of the incident at Western Port. Now I'm not sure that you can rely totally on reports that reach the Governor after transition through five correspondents, none of whom were actually in attendance.

Whether or not the blacks who committed the attacks were led by the virago, Trugannini or whether it was the Sydney negro or even Warrigal himself, is uncertain. Trugannini was in the area, she'd stolen horses and weapons at farms from Melbourne to Port Albert. She'd become so used to the ways of whites in the company of that idiot, Protector Robinson, but whether or not she'd branched out into murder is hard to say. No one ever interviewed my sailors, the authorities knew the dead men were from the *Ocean* but the island we inhabited was only sketchily known, even in those days, and by then Governor Gipps had been promising to hang whites who killed blacks no matter what the reason.

Silence reigned in the Port Phillip district. Trugannini and her band were accused, and probably responsible for the murder, but the thirty-eight Bunurong blacks that my men shot while they slept in their wurrungs probably had no knowledge that any white man had been killed. If so they'd certainly not have allowed themselves to be caught so unawares.

If any of them were the same people that killed my men on Sea Elephant Bay it may never be known, but justice in the eyes of the sailors had been done. Many eyes for an eye.

Thirty-eight. You might be surprised by that number because none so large ever reached La Trobe and even if it had would have remained hidden in his desk while he wrote a more general, innumerate, report to Gipps. La Trobe was a man's man, he looked upon the blacks like apes. We all did. Most of us.

The *Ocean* came back. Another three sailors short, but we never reported that either or they'd be asking questions about the Bunurong and eventually they'd expose the riches we were harvesting on the Bass Strait island.

Silence.

The first act of the men on their return to Sea Elephant Bay was to set fire to the native houses and when the turf had been burnt they pushed over the stone walls. Any return by the blacks, no matter if we were here or not, would not be in such comfort as before, and if they did manage to rebuild it would be at the expense of much labour and at the rate things were going, how much labour could they call on?

We missed Fanny, Belle and Woonaji of course; well I had Eugenie, but it didn't stop me wondering about those lovely creatures and my curiosity in what they knew, the secrets of the sea which, as a sea captain, I resented remaining hidden from me. I dreamt of them, the flash of their wet limbs in the shallows of the bay, the suppleness of their bodies, and no doubt the men had the same disturbing dream because work on the island was surly and intermittent until they captured two women in a canoe on a distant part of the coast while ostensibly seeking out more seal colonies. They didn't even speak the same language as our own women but they were certainly subjected to the same introductory beatings and thereafter the more embittered sexual attentions of the men.

They made cursory attempts to hide much of this from Eugenie but the stiffening set of her jaw made it certain she knew most of the story. Vanderlin came to me with the men's demand that Eugenie not be allowed to visit their women.

She took this news without looking up from the curtain she was sewing but you could see admonition in the quicker, firmer entry and exit of the needle through the coarse gingham we'd brought from England. I would have preferred the Chinese silks, or even the African weaves, but Eugenie stuck to her idea of an Irish cottage.

As the men relaxed into their residence of Sea Elephant Bay the work on the buildings and at the try pots recommenced with more energy and purpose.

We had begun work on a small building which would serve as our home until we could gain the time and resources to build a proper house but Eugenie took only mild interest in any of these plans, a fact I found strange, believing the stories of other men who spoke of their wives' avid domestic materialism. But we took our wine to the bench outside the hut which, despite the interruptions, was all but finished. Briggs, Vanderlin and I had erected most of the structure while West organised the sawing of timber in the pit. The walls were partly lined in sweet smelling dark-red driftwood timbers gathered in a rocky bay on the western side of the island. None of us could recognise the wood and nor were there records of a ship like this having been wrecked in the Strait since we'd begun sealing. There were wrecks of course, scores of them, but between all of us we had sailed on or seen all of them in one port or the other and having laboured on them for days we could pick the idiosyncrasies of their timbers from any other. This ship was unknown, as were the characteristics of its construction. Nevertheless its timbers made fine lining boards.

So, on this particular evening, Eugenie and I were enjoying our wine and the delightful view of the bay afforded by the position I'd selected for our first home when I asked Eugenie a simple question of her afternoon walk to the north end of the island after which I'd seen her in close conversation with West. I wasn't jealous, not at all, I'd simply asked the question as a way of opening a conversation, almost as you would with a stranger, but the sudden guardedness in her manner made me realise she'd never before told me a lie but was contemplating telling one now.

I couldn't believe it had anything to do with West and began to form a second question when she turned fully toward me and put her hand on my own. I wondered if it was the first time she'd touched me voluntarily.

'Caleb, I trust you. I trust very little, have never had cause to, but I trust you and I hope you will deal with the news I am about to give you with the compassion of which I believe you are capable.' I began to struggle with a few words but it probably only sounded like grunts and splutters.

'Caleb,' she resumed, 'one of the native women has been found by West. She was hurt when her boat capsized on the reef while the natives were escaping. West saw the smoke she was sending up as a signal to her fellows. She has a child, Caleb, a very fair child. It's father is probably on this island.'

'Unless he was killed by the blacks – here, or at Western Port.'

'Perhaps, Caleb, but it doesn't matter now. West has been very careful. The woman is in a small cave in the rocks and he's been providing for her.'

'Why?'

'Well, who could answer for West's motivation, Caleb? You seem as much at a loss to explain the fellow as I am. But please, Caleb, I beg you not to tell the others, otherwise I feel I will have betrayed her . . . and West.'

'West?'

'He seems most gentle with her, Caleb.'

'Perhaps he is the father.'

'He says that is impossible, but . . . but he has taken it into his mind to leave the island and take the woman and child with him.'

'Which woman is it?' I asked, blushing suddenly at the thought it could be Belle.

'Woonaji.'

'Woonaji! But she's quite old. And . . . and besides I can't do without West, he's the only one . . .'

'He has a high regard for you, Caleb, he has seen what you have planned here, how you are using your wealth and he has his own earnings from the seals, enough he thinks to . . .'

'West, really, but I'm not sure I can run this place . . .'

'He's asked to borrow the long boat, Caleb.'

'Asked you?'

'Well, no, not asked, just mentioned that he might need some assistance to leave before the men find out. They'd see her as a murderer even if she'd had nothing to do with it . . . and the child, I don't know what they'd do to the child.'

'I'll go with him. We can say we are establishing a base closer to Van Diemen's. Are you happy to remain here for a week or so? Vanderlin and Briggs are crude but they will not harm you and they can control the others. I think it is the only way. If they found her they'd kill her outright. And the child. And with West, I don't know, but it would imperil our work. If they knew we'd been party to it they'd turn on us for sheltering the murderer of their mates.'

'There's no evidence that she . . .'

'They don't need evidence, they need a crime and a victim upon whom to avenge the crime, several victims. We'll go at once. I'll tell them the purpose of our journey. Can you make sure Woonaji and the child are ready to swim out to the boat from the south western point. They'll have to hurry, we'll meet them there around sunset.'

I had no real fear for Eugenie's safety. The men treated her with respect, daunted by her frostiness and remote demeanor. She treated them fairly but that was all. The men were enjoying the rich spoils of our operation and while many of them tossed their money into the hands of the first whores and taverns we came across on our way to the market ports, others like Vanderlin could see that in no time at all they'd be wealthy men. They'd understand immediately West's decision to set out for himself and buy land. He was respected rather than popular and while his ingenuity would be missed we were at a point in our labours where we'd soon be setting sail with a full cargo and would simply have one less pocket amongst which to divide our spoils. They could all add up even if most couldn't read or write.

Two of us could sail the whaleboat Briggs had retrieved from the mud islands off Port Albert. The natives must have realised she would be more trouble for them than it was worth so they abandoned her before it drew the attention of the sheep-walk settlers who had begun pushing into the south-eastern parts of Western Port and beyond.

As West and I set our sail and steered her around Cannon Point and out of sight of our settlement I admired the skills of the natives who had sailed her across to the mainland, never having seen a craft like her. I'd seen them using paddles and small sheets of bark as sails but never anything like our ships. They must have understood the sailing of the craft implicitly because when Briggs found her all the ropes had been wound, the sails lashed to the mast. It was an act of respect, not for us, but for the craft. Instant sailors.

There were plenty who portrayed them as mere monkeys but they were far from that, they were just in the way. Oh, I'm not trying to be holier than thou, they were in our way too. We would never be able to relax if we knew they were in our area. A few guns and they were capable of driving us away . . . so we shot first. Like the McMillans who'd learnt enough of the determination of the Port Phillip tribes to defend their land. They shot first and often. Briggs had heard of a hundred bodies on the shore of the Cunningham Lakes, Vanderlin said more. It might have been bravado or it might have been a blunt tactic against a foe arming itself against us. No one could afford to relax now. We all knew that.

We sailed the whale boat around the southern point of Sea Elephant Bay and brought her hard in against the sandbar at the entrance to the lagoon where furze and salt bush clung low in the salty marsh and from where a dark figure splashed through the shallows toward us and slipped over the gunnels like the shadow of a bird.

I could hear West's low voice and occasionally the piping of the infant, but of Woonaji nothing except on one occasion the briefest flaring of the whites of her eyes as she glanced at me.

I felt no burden at all and as we set the sail for the large island we knew to be to our south, my mood was almost one of elation and I realised how the effort of keeping the men happy had been taxing me, and not only that, the delicate tension between Eugenie and myself was like a grass seed in a sock, and so to sail south was a holiday. I didn't have to do anything but sail, as I'd done all my life, I had no responsibility for West and his companions, in fact I'd sail the return leg on my own. The weight lifted from my heart and I whistled an old American sailing song we'd been taught by some Bostoners. I can hear it still and realise how close it came to the plaintive voice of the sea birds who are, now, my only companions.

'Farewell to Tarwathie
We're ready to sail
On the cruel coast of Greenland
We're hunting the whale
The blue ice above us
The cold sea below
Our eyes on the cruel sea
Awaiting the blow.'

We could have done without the south-easterly, she's a bitter wind in the Strait but we'd seen that before and our craft was built for just this kind of sea, she plunged her head into the waves like the blunt brow of the whales she'd been built to hunt.

On the second day West began muttering to Woonaji who had been gazing at the horizon since first light. Their concentration aroused my curiosity, even suspicion, and I scanned the ocean with the telescope and immediately in line with our bow saw the low rise of an island group and, rising from it, a thin intermittent column of smoke.

I knew from other ships that there were a group of islands off the north-east tip of Van Diemen's but I'd never seen them before and I doubted that West could have been here, as he'd been aboard the *Ocean* for the entire period since the Strait's discovery. He was getting his information from other quarters.

As we approached the island close enough to see the straits between the offshore islets, the mountain range on the main island became defined against the violet blur of the land behind. I noticed that smoke no longer rose and I became uneasy about the inhabitants of the island and my passengers' communication with them.

There was much pointing and gesticulation as we approached a barrier of reef off the main island.

'I've decided I'll try here first,' West declared.

There was only a small gap in the reef and I took us past it in order to inspect the entrance and that's when I saw a boat drawn up on the far end of the beach. I took up the telescope. It was one of the missing long boats from the *Ocean*. I dropped the glass to find West looking at me.

'Some of Woonaji's people come from here. They must have brought the boat across from Westernport. I'll return the boat when I can. Or buy it from you. I have the money.'

'Very well. So, you're living here? With them?'

'Have a look, sir, you've seen the grasslands as we sailed by. The rivers. This is as good a pasture as we've seen.' I'd never heard him call me sir, before, or anyone else for that matter.

'And how would you propose to transport your stock from the markets?'

'We will build a landing. Ships will begin to call.'

'These . . . people, will accept you?'

'I believe so.'

'West, I am sad to lose you. You have been a very good shipman, I'll find it difficult without you.'

'Captain Mathews, you will find it difficult soon enough. You have made all the men enough money, I doubt whether any will return for another season. They'll do what I'm doing, buy up land, those who don't drink themselves to death in Portsmouth or Sydney . . . you'll be looking for another crew, I believe.'

We'd never spoken such long continuous sentences to each other. No storm, no iceberg, no shredded sail had ever called for such complicated talk.

'Well, thank you, West, we've all become rich, it should have occurred to me that others were beginning to think along the same lines as I myself have been doing. And you, of course.'

'If you would take us through the reef, I'd be obliged. What do you want for the boat, sir?'

'I want you to look after it.'

'You won't tell the others, sir, they might . . .'

'I will say nothing. I am concerned at how completely you are cutting yourself off from your countrymen, West.'

'I have no country, sir, I was born at sea.'

'But still, you are English, your country is still . . .'

'This will be country enough for me, sir.'

'And family?'

He didn't reply, merely cast a long gaze across the line of the horizon and the contours of the island to which he'd committed his life.

'If you could take us to the beach, sir, I'd be obliged.'

Inside the reef was a bay barely large enough for the whale boat to turn about, only small vessels could trade with this island. It would be a small economy.

West and Woonaji with the child, waded to the shore, and only West raised a hand before they disappeared in the tea-tree scrub which lined the shore.

I re-negotiated the entrance but found myself strangely reluctant to return immediately to Sea Elephant. West was as close to being a friend as I'd ever had. His departure discomfited me because without him my control of the *Ocean*'s operation would be far more precarious.

I amused myself by sailing amongst the numerous reefs and islands to the north and east of West's island but on passing the largest of three, perhaps less than half a mile from the mother island, I again saw smoke and scanning the shore with the glass I spied two women, black women, fishing in the rock pools.

My sail was close reefed for the purpose of the delicate negotiation, so it would take a vigilant eye to spy my boat from the shore.

It was difficult steering the craft close in to the reefs and using the glass at the same time but something made my purpose seem urgent. And you'll think of one primary urgent purpose, of course, and my mind did savour the thought of those wet limbs, but one of the women in particular seemed familiar, the way she carried herself, the ebullience of her manner . . .

Belle. It was Belle and perhaps, Fanny, but the glass hovered as if by itself on the gorgeous form of Belle. She was a beauty, it has to be said. Sailors can be lured by sirens who turn out to be seals and so, we seamen, can be unreliable in the discernment of beauty after too long at sea, but Belle lingered in my dreams because she was truly beautiful. And for me, dangerously irresistible.

You might say I should have been circumspect, more alert, you might say I should have been less controlled by base desire, but I will say that it was not base desire, it was certainly carnal but I continue to maintain that my intentions were neither simply lascivious nor entirely selfish. I believed and still believe, even after all that has happened, that between Belle and I there was . . . a hint of understanding . . . a hint . . .

At any rate events, as always, took charge of them-selves.

I ground the bow of the whaleboat into the coarse, sloping sand of the shore, heedless of her dangerous list, calling as I went, but I'd no sooner caught her on threat of the gun I carried, yes you will argue that the presence of the firearm coloured my intention, but I'll maintain that no seaman of that era would venture ashore without one.

The first spear caught me just below the collarbone. I had hold of Belle's arm so I dragged her toward me and retreated to the boat knowing I could only afford one shot of the weapon. How familiar with firearms were these people? Belle's presence would mean they had to be aware of some of our advantages.

We clambered aboard the boat as best I could with the spear in my arm. Belle knew firearms so I pushed the muzzle into her face and she quieted immediately. A wave lifted the bow of the whaleboat and broadside as she was, she attempted to follow the retreating wave and I had just enough time to drop the firearm, grab the gaff and pole her into deeper water. The natives were emboldened by my release of the gun and swarmed down the beach and let go a volley of spears, some of which hit us abeam, the wind of others lashed my cheek and thigh, but I had the gun again and released it into the most advanced warrior who fell back into the shore's wash, his arm folding over his escaping intestines.

The other warriors howled and disappeared behind rocks, trees, scrub, any cover they could find. Obviously they were too unfamiliar with guns to realise I had no hope of re-loading if they should attack again immediately.

I poled us into the deeper water and then set the sail as quickly as I could, the spear still hanging from my arm. I caught Belle's glance at the shore and saw a canoe being launched and I slumped in the stern, re-loaded the weapon and pretended to be wrestling with the sheets.

The warriors got within the range of their spears but the heavy gauge ball from the gun caught them both, blasting them from the canoe. Belle hid her face in her arms.

Again I reloaded the weapon and turned it upon her.

'Take the spear out,' I said. She feigned ignorance but I menaced with the gun and held out my knife. Her eyes told me she knew exactly what had to be done.

She sawed at the shaft. It was dark, hard wood like hickory and the sawing put pressure on the shaft and I prayed I would not faint because if I did I knew I'd never wake.

Belle released the barb, a razor-sharp flint embedded in a slot of the spear, and as I withdrew the shaft blood rushed from the wound, but I'd seen many accidents at sea and soon had it staunched, all the while reflecting on how few seconds were required to change a man's life forever. I'd killed a man again, three men, and now I'd kidnapped a woman.

I know you'll scoff and ask about all the other women we'd stolen from various parts of the coast but I rationalised it then, and still believe there is some truth in the fact, that I had merely acquiesced to the power of the men's appetites, that to refuse them this liberty would have placed my own life in danger.

I would not have removed the women myself . . . but, of course, I availed myself of them once they were part of our company, but how many men would not have done so? And I treated them better than the others. Belle in particular. With Belle it was not just lust, although if you'd seen her you would have known the temptation.

You're right, of course, I can feel your scorn beyond the page, it's a flimsy justification, but in the safety of your distance in leagues and years, don't think we were all brutes.

Perhaps that's what we've become. If you were to see me, and I'm sure you won't, you would probably dismiss me as some . . . but it's too late for that. The couple of hundred seconds that elapsed between grabbing Belle's arm and shooting the warriors had changed my life irrevocably, a life I had imagined was on the point of becoming more sedate than that of a sea captain, more civilised than that of a sealer and more respectable than either.

She had her face turned away but I could feel her revulsion.

'Belle. Belle, I'm sorry. I had no idea the men would attack like that. I was just coming to talk to you.' The merest hint of a shrug, or scorn.

'Believe me, Belle, I didn't mean to harm you. I've missed you.' I wasn't sure she would have understood much of what I said but that only allowed me a freedom of speech I'd never known.

'Remember fishing at Sea Elephant Bay? Remember cooking the crayfish and mullet, Belle? We shared them, remember? I loved those nights. I've sometimes imagined that . . .' I wasn't really sure what I had imagined beyond some hectic images and some impossibly domestic ones. A white man and a black woman. How could an Englishman live like that? It was all right for West. As he said himself, he was virtually stateless, virtually without a history of any kind.

So we sailed like that for two days. She never looked directly at me. The sulphur powder we always kept in a waterproof chest along with wax, thread and canvas rendered my shoulder numb but, after bathing the wound every four hours in salt water, I could tell that no infection had taken hold and re-applied the sulphur, more confident in having escaped death by poisoning.

On the third night I showed the gun to Belle and pressed her into the boards of the hull and she neither moved nor let me see her face. It was even less satisfac-

tory than those few occasions I allowed myself at Sea
Elephant Bay. She had more reason to hate me now and
it did nothing to rid me of the feeling that the careful
design of my life was unravelling, in fact on all three
occasions I took her like that my heart plunged deeper
into the trough.

She'd hardly spoken a word but after the final
humiliation she drew a scrap of canvas about her and
challenged me.

'Shoot, amerjie, shoot poor woman. You wan'
woman, you wan' land, you wan' kurrman, you wan' all
plurry ocean. You big amerjie, you big man, I spit you
guli, amerjie, I spit you eye, you not warrior, you boy,
you shitty arse boy, I spit you, I plurry spit all you mob,
I . . .' At last the denunciation was swallowed by sobs,
but she'd already disabused me of any pastoral notion
of two people at either end of a fishing net in a calm bay
at evening. That dream of unity between man and
woman, black and white evaporated forever if, under
these circumstances, it had ever been conceivable.

And now, within sight of the hummock of Sea
Elephant Bay, what did I think I was going to do with
her? The men would recognise her immediately, for the
same reason I had, but in possession of other women
they would not allow lust from preventing them killing
one who they believed had betrayed them and
murdered their fellows.

I took the boat further to the east and passed the
island beyond their sight and later that afternoon I
released her on a sandbar close enough to the shore of
Port Albert so that she could wade ashore.

Now, as I indicated for her to leave the boat, she did
look at me, wading backwards through the water until
she reckoned she was out of range and then she turned
and ran, plunging where the channels were deeper and
all the time the lowering western sun made her body
magnificent, mythic. Few are the nights since when that
image has not disturbed my sleep.

Perhaps women and most men think it is just lust,

that any body is good enough, but you are wrong to think that. For some men images of that kind shape their lives and when they sleep that is what they see, that body and no other. Women call it love, I would not know, but for men it is blindness and their sight only returned to them in sleep, unless of course, she shares the same bed. But there again I would not know.

My return to Sea Elephant was not as welcoming as I'd conjured it during the years of planning and scheming for my ideal island base. I was disconcerted by the turn events had taken on the southern island and began to suspect that I may have picked up a dose of venereal. A mess, the whole thing had been a mess, not the release from captain's duties I'd imagined, and complicated by the fact that West was no longer on our island to lend his immense practicality to my project.

Eugenie was attentive in her dutiful manner but I felt strongly that she suspected some of the things which had occurred.

The injury to my arm was easy enough to explain as spear heads were still embedded in the beam timbers, but my explanation of the attack sounded hollow to my ears and perhaps that lie was translated to my eyes because Eugenie seemed to stiffen in her guardedness even more than usual.

Vanderlin and Briggs had lined and floored the cabin and we ate our evening meal at a table made of planks. The freshly sawn timber had a beautiful aroma and sitting at the table we could look down over the harbour where the *Ocean* rode a placid anchor.

The wine began to ease some of the tension I had been feeling and in an attempt to further dispel my misgivings I drew Eugenie to me and, as gently as I could manage, I unbuttoned her gown. She blushed fiercely and perhaps I should have known that the romance of the twilight was still too much light for the embarrassment we suffered in our coupling.

Eugenie's body was square and rather stiff, the imminent revelation of her breasts was exciting, but in the light, and it is true that I'd never seen them so, they looked rather small and functional, not at all as buoyant and provocative as the fruits of Belle.

Altogether it slowed my arousal and had us in a cumbersome wrestle that took an excruciating length of time. Afterwards the gulf between us seemed even larger than before. The light, the half light, had revealed that the duty of intimacy, the duty we had made of physical love, to be too awkward, too comical to sustain.

Not long after, I was aware of the symptoms of the venereal and the coldness and agitation of Eugenie made me wonder if I had infected her also.

In October of that year we sent off what most of us believed to be our last cargo. It was unacknowledged between us but most of the men had made up their mind to find a softer form of existence using the gains from the bounty of the seal.

Eugenie had arranged to visit the doctor at the Van Diemen port of George Town and I was relieved to have the duty of the *Ocean* to take me on to Sydney and then to Canton or whatever port was most anxious for our services. Medical help of the kind I required was a specialty of such ports.

Looking down on the familiar activity of the dock as we left the Tamar estuary I marvelled at what had been built there in such a short time. I took Collins to Port Phillip in '03 and George Town had not been established for another two years and yet, a mere three years later, there was a substantial and well planned village. And I was sailing away from it and my wife who had come to cure herself of my disease. The knowledge of my betrayal was palpable between us and yet we'd been unable to speak of it or perhaps it was my inability to fashion the words to ease the way for my confession.

Confess. What could I confess? I felt I had not betrayed her at all. Oh, I know you will scoff, but it seemed to me that Eugenie and Belle were not even of the same species, and that is in no way flattering to Eugenie. She is dead you know, just recently, so that knowledge cannot hurt her any more than it had done during her life.

I did not mean ill to her, I would have done anything for her regard, because she was a good woman, and there was a time when she believed in my goodness.

I have come to believe that we are sent to our judgment, not by God, but by those who truly love us and that is why I am using the log of this, my last ship, my light ship, to confess what I have come to know of myself.

Two
TAMAR

This journal is neither complaint nor boast. It will not be a lady's diary nor will it be an attempt at elision to make the life more acceptable or romantic. This is simply as close to the truth as I can get and it's for you Johnny Mullagh, I want you to know about the state of my heart.

People will think, Johnny, that I removed to George Town to escape the infidelity of my husband, Caleb Mathews. That is not the case. I was aware that he had brought the curse upon us both but I neither blamed nor absolved him of his liaison with the black woman.

I was not good at love and neither was he, but he had the greater need. The last years of my life in Ireland had delivered me of any further need in that regard and had left in its place a horror I could neither banish nor hide, so the venereal was not the greatest curse that could have been brought to my door. The door was already shut.

My father was a good man. More than you can say

for most men. He read to me. Sang to me. Sat me in front of his saddle. He spooned porridge into my mouth and set my arm when it was broken in the Battle of Kerry. His tears splashed on my arm as he splinted and bound it with the tenderness of a nun. 'For you, my dear, and your mother,' he muttered all the while, 'I did it for you. I could see no other way, but you can see how they see me. I am disgraced, my darlin', and for that I am sorry. I love you, Eugenie, I love you dearly, I loved you since I saw your eyes when you was born in . . .'

Well, it took some time to set the arm and I blacked in and out and all the while he talked of the troubles and the part he had played and how it had turned out the way it did. I was only twelve, you see, and I struggled to piece together the bits and pieces I heard with the little I knew of the politics of my nation.

He was dead the next morning. Even then I knew I'd lost not just a father but a better friend than I could ever expect to know. A better heart than most men will ever possess. But even so, a flawed heart. That is why I don't feel badly about Caleb. He was a good man, but just a man, struggling within his capacity to make sense of all that befell him; his physical self, his fortune, his new country and the ghost of the old that haunted us both. Johnny, you will die in your country no matter what else happens, but Caleb and myself were cast from ours, never underestimate the affect that has on a person. You've lost your country, I know, that is obvious, but they can never stop you from dying in it, even if they hasten to bring it about.

I can tell you no more than that. It is all I know. In reading the history I could place my father here and Caleb's parents there but it would be just speculation. In the turmoil that preceded and followed my father's death nothing could be seen clearly enough to provide event with reason.

And not long after that I was at Skomer and soon after that at Sea Elephant Bay.

I said the truth, Johnny, but I lied. In those last days

in Kerry something did happen, but even now I struggle to speak of it.

What is courage in a man, Johnny? Or a woman? What is goodness? Is it courageous to fling yourself at the barricade for the honour of your country knowing you will orphan your child and widow your wife? Valour, that's what they call it in books. Or perhaps it is courageous to swallow your pride and principles, corrupt your own heart for the sake of those you love. Most of us do what we know to be right, but then there are some who don't. Some who wait for the relaxation of normal human values and then pounce to release their bestiality. What is constrained and frustrated in peace is a blunt and selfish weapon in war.

The night after they killed my father, and Caleb's, they came back.

'Traitor,' they yelled outside our house. 'Traitors, parasites, orange crawlers.'

I was a girl. The only men I'd known were my father and uncles, the men of Caleb's family. I was innocent, not just in my body, but in my mind. I knew of no evil until that night. Oh, I knew that the wolf ate the lamb and the spider ate the fly, my father had read me these stories but they were never set in our land, never in Ireland, always in some dark, far-off place where it was not uncommon for evil to dwell.

I heard my mother scream but after a time, nothing, and then they came for me, one after another. Big men, spitting at me, crude fingers at me, and then they did it, one after another. Laughing.

When I regained consciousness my body was on fire. I hurt everywhere, they'd broken my arm again, I had blood on me everywhere – and worse.

I crawled to my mother's room. She was still alive, still conscious, but we couldn't meet each other's eyes. I tried at first, tried to seek comfort in her arms, but the depth of her shame quelled my spirit and imprisoned her heart. The women of our family are like that. She died a few days later, but we never spoke again. Can you imagine that, Johnny? Of course, I'm sorry, of course you know what it's like. I wasn't thinking, too immersed in my own story.

But it changed me, Johnny, chilled me, made me incapable of those emotions women are supposed to represent. I'm warning you, Johnny, don't let the cruelty steal the heart out of your chest. Don't let the ignorance of others rob your life of its living soul.

It was all for an idea about freedom, an idea about honour and expressed in its crudest form by people who had never known the emergence of an idea in their brain. That's what makes the leaders so culpable, they know that if they could drum, literally drum, an idea into the mind of the pack, sing it, re-inforce it with the freedom drum, the pack would go wild with the liberty to reveal the sewer of their soul, all in the pusuit of someone else's idea, commit deeds which professors of music and doctors of philosophy will deem necessities of the moment, courageous acts for the cause, professors and philosophers who will compose music to celebrate it, write treatises to justify it, but never a song will they write, Johnny, of a young girl covered in her own blood and the semen of brutes. Never that, Johnny, always a light on the hill, a bugle call, a drum, a flag raised on a hill, never a girl doused in blood and semen.

You'll read about it, one day, the parallel will interest you.

Independence from the oppressors is what they called it. Our family hated the English as much as any Irishman. Why wouldn't you? But when the fight in our town could only be a fight to the death there were some men who looked at the woman in their arms, perhaps they woke and saw a coil of hair lovely against their wife's throat and thought to themselves, I can not, perhaps they crept into their daughter's bedroom and smelt her innocence, saw the painfully childish face on the pillow, and said to themselves, no, no idea is worth that.

And so they sought to make a deal with the army,

the English army, not to become loyalist, certainly not, but to lay down their arms, to live beneath the yoke. Oh, some of them may have been cowards, some may have been craven, selling boots to the British, biscuits to John Bull, who knows? But I'd seen my father and uncles fight, they'd lost sons and still they fought, but at the point where all was about to be lost, they said no, sought to make a deal, but one amongst them must have let the secret known or perhaps the slavering dogs, the whelps of the republic, perhaps they could smell conciliation in the air, couldn't spell it, but they could smell it and couldn't tolerate any idea outside the black and white squares in their brain that passed for thought.

The last resort of the scoundrel: nationalism, border protection, purity of race, God save the Queen, Ireland for the Free. You read it, Johnny, you'll understand, it's happening still.

At what point can a perfectly decent human being accept the death of an innocent as a necessary act in the pursuit of an idea? Women of the church? Men of the Lodge? People of the Empire? It is that point at which you can convince some brute to perform the unthinkable act to implement the idea your fine mind, your gentle religion, your genteel art has created and revered.

I know they say I'm cold, Johnny, I know they say I'm peculiar, but it's because I have no faith, my love, no belief that the goodness of the human spirit will prevail. At least that's what I thought until I saw you as a child, as an innocent robbed of his innocence, and I rallied, determined not to let it happen in another land, not to let the brutes rape another country, let them bring all wealth unto themselves on the pretext of religion, chosen race, freedom and national pride.

I knew you, Johnny, had the spirit to resist and that's why I took you as my son when they killed your mother. Because you were good, Johnny. Are you still?

Well, that is why I write to you, to let you know those things you may not know, put things in a perspective which may help you make sense of a universe you've always struggled to correct. To protect.

So let's begin at the beginning. With what people perceive as my greatest shame. Belle had his child, you see. Oh, I knew of her. Well, it was impossible not to as Belle called the child Gertrude Mathews. There was no escaping knowledge of her. You'll remember her, I know you will. She came over to George Town from time to time and later she was at the school but even though she was older than you, I know you'll remember her. She's over at Port Albert now, had a child, Caleb, so I hear . . .

Anyway, I'm ahead of myself. The first few weeks in George Town were a nightmare. The doctor I'd come to see could barely look in my eyes let alone examine me, so I left in exasperation and found out about a convict woman whose earlier trade had made her an expert in the disease. Meanwhile the doctor made sure that everyone in the town knew what ailed me, so you can imagine the kind of reception I got. The first few landladies I saw would not even give me a room. Never mind that, it was a trifle, for I knew I would have to find a way of employing myself in George Town. Not because Caleb hadn't provided for me well enough, but I had to have a purpose. Not as a reason for not return-ing to Sea Elephant Bay, but so I could stay sane.

Even with my reputation it was obvious that there were things required in the town and not enough people to do them so that even a disgraced and, as they thought, abandoned wife could open a milliner's shop, or run a boarding house or even a school. Children everywhere and no school.

Mr Hull was the self-proclaimed mayor of the town. He had been appointed Justice of the Peace or Magistrate, I can't remember now what he called himself, but you see he was barely literate so it wasn't too hard to impress him with my credentials. I could read and write, skills which impressed him mightily, even though he'd die before admitting it. I was sharp enough to make the most of my advantage by showing him official documents meant to be my qualifications.

He was such a pompous old fool, but so quick and rapid with the blather that he managed to convince many of skills he did not own. I used the same device on him, flashing my Sunday School Certificate for Communion, mightily impressive with its scrolls and curlicues. Latin always looks good on a page and Protestants can't read it, so it helped a great deal.

Perhaps there was too much to be gained by starting a school for him to worry too much about qualifications when there was only one applicant.

The sticky moment came when I told him that I was going to take over the Wesleyan School which had been abandoned by the mission just before I arrived. Some of the students were still boarded there and some were black.

'Surely not, Mrs Mathews, I imaged a rather more refined sort of college. It would be nothing to move the blacks up the river. They're better off out of town and there are more and more children whose parents can pay, don't you see? It'd take you no time to repay my loan.' He owned the Wesleyan School, of course, as he owned most of what stood in the town. He was what they called a self-made man. I was curious as to what he had made himself from because there were many in Van Diemen's who managed to keep the base metal well concealed. This is the man who dominated the entire northern part of Van Diemen. No wonder it became the country it did.

As I insisted on caring for the remaining students his face went purple before he calmed himself in order to give me the benefit of his erudition and common sense, the sense of a self-made man.

'You see, Mrs Mathews, I believe that all attempts to Christianise them will prove ineffectual, and I refer to a much higher authority than mine, the authority of some very eminent men of all classes of missionary, from the first Roman Catholic Mission down to Mr Dredge and Mr Robinson. I believe that it is the design of Providence that the inferior races should pass away before the superior races, and that independently of all other causes, since we have occupied the country, the aborigines must cease to occupy it.'

It was on the tip of my tongue to ask if he also thought that of the Irish, but he was just a monkey. Imagine a monkey dressed in black velvet with red, military style braiding, court shoes, stern glasses and a meerschaum pipe, a monkey who had been taught to prate platitudes and attitudes and to believe that they had arisen from his own intelligence. That was Mr William Hull, esquire, a catalyst in an antipodean experiment to prove that in any society the ambitious dross rises to the top of the cauldron.

They despised me of course, only ever invited me to their social occasions when they couldn't avoid it. Such as when the commoners, like Mrs Kennedy, the school housekeeper, were deemed worthy of an invitation.

I suppose most of them believed I would be cut by their denial of me but in fact it was for such things my life had prepared me. You'll hear a lot of gab from Irishmen about being outcast and siding with the oppressed. Well that is true, unless of course the oppressed are black or Chinese, then even an Englishman becomes good company for most Irish. But you know all that.

This new society was as class conscious as any I'd known. The new rich strove to cement their good fortune by commandeering preferences to land grants and trading licenses at the expense of those less fortunate and, of course, your people were considered slaves at best, an unwanted species at worst.

The whole incredible range of human sentiment was displayed here. There were occasions, and I know it for a fact because your grandmother told me, that men rode back into town as heroes after the slaughter of a whole clan of Palewa people, and were received in glory, garlanded, yes, I saw it, women throwing garden flowers in their path, taken into the public houses and their triumphs lauded as a great advance for the district. Later, after Governor Bourke arrived in Sydney, they had to be more circumspect because he was trying to protect your people and halt the advance of the frontier.

And that's when your mother was killed.

1830. The school had been opened for twenty-two years. A long time, but even so we were still capable of a bestiality no history of Imperial England allows.

Now, Johnny, you must not allow my stories and your own knowledge to lead you into thinking that every English, Scottish and Irish person was a brute.

George Town had been chosen by the men because of the great Tamar River and the agricultural lands that opened from it but it was built by women. Oh, the stones were cut by men, the timbers sawn and the windows glazed by men, the streets made, the wharf built, but it was the women who transformed it.

If you walk around it today, look around. How sunny and mild are the days in this town? What a place to rear children. What a place to educate them.

The regular streets lead you to water whichever way you walk, roses lean over fences, honeysuckle climbs walls, benches are built where the view is just right. It is benign, Johnny, even after all that has happened there are spirits at work here in love with beauty, and what greater recommendation can you give the human spirit?

Any evening you would find me walking those streets to sit on the very benches I've mentioned, exulting in the sweet perfumes of the gardens, the quiet sanctity of the harbour and the dolorous lassitude of that heavenly climate. George Town was a town built by men but shaped by women with a dream of Eden in their minds.

The boats turning their bows into the tide as they ride so gently at anchor, the children with their mothers picking oysters and mussels from the rocks, the dogs gamboling in the water, the sun's rich blood suffusing the evening sky. We are not all brutes, Johnny, don't ever let yourself believe that we are. George Town is a creation of the truly civilised part of our soul.

1830, of course, was but one example of the other face of the King's coin.

Where are you now, Johnny? I hope you are alive, we haven't heard a word from you since you went to Victoria. Up on the Murray, so I've been told by Aunty Ida.

Well, I do hope you can read this because this is what happened to your mother. You never asked before and I never told. Perhaps I thought it wouldn't be a useful knowledge for you to have, but what a thing for a schoolteacher to think. What use is knowledge hidden?

1830. Governor Arthur thought he was doing his Christian duty, or so he always said, but in fact he was doing what the great new egalitarian society demanded. Getting rid of the blacks. The Pied Piper, Robinson, turned up just at the right, or you would say wrong, time.

They always said only two were killed at the Fence of Legs but no one ever mentioned Mr Burbury who died of heart attack trying to climb over a log, and of course no one counted your mother.

1830, October 7. Every man in the colony went completely silly with excitement. What a lark, what an adventure! Boys with sticks, men with guns, old men with dogs that hadn't left the front gate for five years, everyone wanted to be in on the fun.

You could hear them beating the bushes as they went, laughing and joking, singing any military song of which they could remember more than a couple of words and half the tune. We never knew what went on when we couldn't hear them anymore but back in town there was an eerie silence. Women clustered together whispering about the great adventure. I am sure that some would have wondered about the morality of it, wondered what Christ on the cross would have made of it, but there had been so much violence, much of it hearsay, and all the women were half off their heads with the vision of their murder by a black hand. And worse. That's what all the whispering was about. Outrage it was. Outrage. Worse than a shark attack.

And these were the same women who trained honeysuckle up the walls and angled their chairs into the path of the sun.

It must have occurred to one of them that not all blacks were behind the barrier. 'What about old Tom, the oyster picker, he's black, isn't he?' 'Yes, but he lives in the town, or on the beach anyway.' 'You buy his oysters, Florrie,' one of them would have said. 'But he's black all the same,' another Christian would have replied. 'Well, what about Dilly Mullagh, then, she's black too.'

I felt the town's eyes turn on the school and the maid who worked in the kitchen and dormitories. Nothing was said but there was plenty of whispering on corners and the casting of glances over shoulders when any of the school community went by.

Everyone knew Dilly. At one time or another every child at the school, and that meant every child at the settlement, had their nose wiped or their shoes tied by your mother. She was an instinctively kind woman, especially to children, but what could she do with adults, they acted as if she didn't exist.

She arrived at George Town already pregnant with you. One morning she was just there. Probably dumped by a sealing vessel. Well, those men were terrible, she was lucky not to have been tipped overboard or left on an uninhabited reef as others were.

One morning she was just there. I suppose she would have taken up with the local clans eventually but she was so close to birth that she had no hope of travelling, apart from the fact that she could hardly stand after such a long period at sea. At any rate she ended up at the school. The minister's wife virtually hunted her into our garden. And you were born a few hours later.

Oh, you were alright. Bellowed for about twenty seconds and then drank like a sailor. But Dilly was bleeding badly, in a terrible state. We would just get it under control and then it would start again, with her lapsing in and out of consciousness while you drank or slept. Thank goodness you were such a good baby.

That went on for about a week but gradually your mother began to improve. She had one of those woven baskets with her. That's all she had. A dilly bag. That's what we called her. I'm ashamed of that now but it was a name that just stuck. Everyone called her Dilly, never anything else.

And in that bag she had a florin and a halfpenny and a bunch of herbs tied with a kind of string. Once, when she woke, she motioned for me to give her the dilly bag and she just took out the weeds and ate them, just like that.

'Thank you, missus,' she said, 'Old Man Weed, plenny good bye an' bye.' And she was. Improved within hours.

I honestly can't say how she came to stay. Well she was still very weak for months after the childbirth but somehow or other no one seemed to consider that she would leave. Mrs Kennedy was very keen for her to stay. Not just because she needed some help with the cooking and cleaning but as you know, Johnny, and most don't, Mrs Kennedy's own mother was off a sealing boat. Violet was so kind to your mother, treated her like a sister. And so your mother never left.

There were always Palewa people about. There was always someone coming in to see Mrs Kennedy, always someone leaving with a bag of food, and people came to see Dilly too. Relatives mostly, I suppose. I didn't know how that worked, we never seemed to know who was related to whom. I'm ashamed of how ignorant I was in those days but I would plead that, for a woman on her own running the only school in the whole district, I had enough to do, never enough time to learn the things I wanted to learn.

1830. You were only about nine or ten, I suppose.
But you know that. One of your uncles, or whatever he
said he was, came to get you a couple of days before,
pleaded with Dilly and Mrs Kennedy to go with him but
no, they stayed, and you, I didn't know where you went
at that time. Aunty Ida says you were on the island
birding and fishing but I knew nothing and then after
Dilly's death I had no way of knowing and Mrs
Kennedy had to be careful, very careful.

The men came back from the line and they were
half ashamed. I suppose they expected to come back as
heroes, marching the prisoners along in front of them,
receiving the plaudits of the town for their heroism and
citizenship but there were none. No prisoners. So there
was a sort of emptiness for them. I don't really know
how it happened, we certainly never knew who did it or
why. All we could do was guess. Perhaps the deflation
of having been so humiliated caused such resentment
that when they saw your mother she appeared as the
symbol of all their frustrations. The gossip of the women
wouldn't have helped, probably goaded the men to
relieve the wounds to their pride, whatever, it only
meant one thing. They killed your mother.

Mrs Kennedy found her, and her scream, she only
screamed once, had me running down the stairs. She'd
been badly beaten about the head, broken arms, one
broken leg, she wouldn't have had a hope.

And they probably did even worse to her. You
might not want to know the details, but how am I to
know? I don't have long myself, Johnny, that's why I'm
so desperate to see you, you were like my child after
that, weren't you? So, you see, I have to tell it all,
because what if that is the thing you wanted to know
and you pick up this journal and it's not there? I have to
tell it all. I'm sorry if it is upsetting. You were always
such a sensitive boy, always loved your mother so much,
loved all of us. The school prospered while you were
with us, Johnny, it always seemed such a happy place.

So we didn't see you again for what was it, six

years. Aunty Ida says that uncle of yours was her husband's father, Bung Eye Armstrong, Bungey everyone called him, that's how he introduced himself to me in 1836 when he brought you back from that dreadful island. Well, at least he brought you back, hardly anyone else survived it. I heard a little bit from Aunty Ida about the hell it became. Sometimes your aunt can get carried away with her own stories, but others I've spoken to, the more sympathetic citizens, were horrified by what they saw over there. Captain Scott, for instance, he had the *Argonaut*, you remember, traded amongst all those islands, he began to tell me of the despair of the Palewa up there at Wybalena but he couldn't continue for the choking of his voice and the tears in his eyes, 'Mrs Mathews, they sit every day looking south towards their home, it is the most dispiriting thing I have ever seen.'

You never told me anything about the island, Johnny. Some say you were on Robinson's prison, others say you lived like pirates. You never said and when you and Uncle Bung Eye came back to George Town you were both in chains, of course.

You must never think that all white men and women have evil at the centre of their hearts. You are partly white yourself, Johnny. But perhaps you have learned about the hearts of men, perhaps not. It was Captain Scott, I believe, who helped you on the islands and if it hadn't been for him I don't know what they would have done to you.

He argued, he pleaded, he threatened. But the crowd was stony-faced. They were blaming you for the death of Hamish Black out at Devonport. That's another thing I know nothing about. He argued all that day and at the end of it they gave you back to me and they took Uncle Bung Eye to Hobart and hung him.

Captain Scott was devastated. It ruined his health. He felt that Bungey's death was his own fault. I tried to assure him of the good he had done but he just stood up from the chair in the parlour and said, 'Eugenie, I virtually traded old Bungey for the boy. It may as well have been me who sentenced him to death.'

You may not have wanted to know that either, but as I wrote before, how am I to know what you'll regret I've included or condemn me for leaving out.

Captain Scott was never the same. I only saw him on two other occasions and it was like watching a man disappear before you. He's buried on Hummock Island. Aunty Ida says the people buried him in their way, smoke and what have you. They saw him for what he was, the soul of Christian kindness, so you must remember white people like that, Johnny. You see, I'm asking you to remember me like that too because I did what I could, it's just that so few of us have control over the events that rush upon our lives.

When you came back from the islands you must have been, what, fourteen? It was never the same. Everyone treated you like a man, a black man. You were so strong and capable that even we forgot you were still just a boy. Got you cleaning the gutters and fixing the doors, things we'd convinced ourselves only a man could do. Oh, you didn't seem to mind, you loved all the tools and things, you were so clever with your hands, and I still taught you at night. You were so tall, too big to be sitting with the littlies, but you didn't need much time anyway. So quick you were with your reading and writing. I suppose that's where part of the problem was. Any old people still about were always asking you to write letters for them to the Governor, permission to get their children back, requests to work on a particular property, asking for help because a fisherman had worked them for two seasons and not paid them a penny. That was Adams, wasn't it? Old Bob Adams, he was such a wicked man, his heart overflowing with hate and contempt.

We are not all like that, Johnny. I know that you loved me, loved all of us, but you must learn to love others too, there are some who mean you no harm.

Not too many in George Town, though, I agree.

Because you were always up a ladder or writing letters to the Governor on behalf of your people, the town, like us, looked on you as a man. A black man. Any small theft, any assault on a woman, the magistrate was around to see you. We were always looking over our shoulder. You must have got sick of it too. Having to explain yourself all the time, having to be responsible for your people, and still only a boy, but so big, Johnny, that was half the trouble, treated like a man, blamed like a man.

One day stays in my mind, Johnny, one day where, for the first time, I felt like I knew the country. Why hadn't it happened before this? Surrounded by all that beauty, not just the honeysuckle and the arbors, but the grandeur of the Tamar itself, even Sea Elephant, why hadn't I seen it before, why hadn't it called me? Because I was denying it? I didn't feel like I was denying the land, it's not as if I was continually pining for Ireland. I'd left there knowing I was stateless, that I'd never return, but why did it take so long for me to fall in love, Johnny?

You may not even remember the day. The school had a little boat by then. Mrs Kennedy used it to get the mussels and oysters from the sandbar in front of the school. Remember how she used to tuck her skirts into her bloomers and reef at the oars with such strength? Sometimes seeing her out there at dusk, silhouetted against the sunset, you could really see the blackness of her. Oh, your people saw it straight away of course, but it surprised me how so few of the townspeople noticed, considering how sensitive they were about the presence of any black people in the town.

Anyway, school was finished for the year and we took the boat across the river to where Beauty Point is now. Nothing over that side in those days except that sandbank and behind it another little river and in one of its tributaries that waterfall. Oh, I wish I could know if you remember it, Johnny.

We fished with handlines and caught six of the

biggest flathead I've ever seen. Beauties they were. I'd hardly ever held a line before but you were so patient with me and then you made a sort of creel out of grass and left the fish tied to the bow to keep them fresh. You seemed to know so much. Your time on the islands, I suppose.

And then you showed me the little waterfall where it cascaded between a crowd of ferns into the river. You swam right in to it and the fall plunged onto your head. Did my eyes tell you know transfixed I was by that? I can't remember us saying much to each other all through that day. But you said this, Johnny, I'll remember it until I die.

'Ma,' you said, 'why don't you swim, the water's not deep. I'll go around the bend and get more bait. Swim, Ma, put your head in the water.' And then you said the thing which changed me forever. 'It's a blessing, Ma, it's a consecration. If you do that the country will baptise you.'

How old were you, Johnny? Fourteen? And speaking like a priest or a prophet. Oh, how your country wasted you, Johnny, what it missed by never seeing past the blackness of your face.

And you swam off to collect the bait, and I did what I thought unthinkable. You had commanded it by your good reason. I took off my clothes, even the underclothes, and stepped into the water hiding myself with my hands from the forest and the lorikeets and then let myself sink below the water. Oh that feeling, Johnny, that weightlessness. That release. I'd never swum before, and even though I was half terrified I crept up to the fall and let the river bless me.

How can you explain the thunder on your head, the rush of cold over your face, the immersion? It was such a simple thing. Poke your head out of the fall and you're back into the sun and the air, draw yourself back into the cascade and you are obliterated. Obliterated may not be quite right. Subsumed? Humbled? Effaced? But you were right. A blessing.

I found I could breathe within the fall. If I was careful. Little pockets of air where the water divided and left a tiny chamber for your nose and mouth, just enough to gasp at life, just enough to allow you to stay immersed, gulping like a fish.

I swam back to the boat. Well, not like you, I suppose it was more of a crawl because I couldn't swim, but it didn't matter, I was different, I understood the water – and how could you live by so much of it and completely deny its existence? I never looked on the country in the same way again.

I'd turn a corner of the town and catch a glimpse of the estuary and feel the water rushing past my ears and lips, I'd gulp at the air and it seemed to me that I understood what the land was asking of me. Thank you, Johnny.

Was it still in my eyes? Anyway, you rowed me up and down the river, underneath the golden wattles reaching over the water, into the tiniest creeks where the bream were clustered around the fallen logs like Christians in a church, you showed me the goanna slip off the bank and lie on the bottom, waiting for us to go, taking sanctuary in the water.

The day stretched out in a long glide of serene bow and dipping oar and I returned to the school with a softness on my heart, a comfort I cannot remember having felt before. People will laugh, Johnny, if they could read this, Christians don't actually believe in epiphanies, the road to Damascus is just a place to bargain for statuettes and jewellery, but I hope you read it, so that you can know what that day meant. Oh, how your country wasted you, Johnny, the opportunity they missed.

And how we wasted the country, Johnny. I'm ashamed to tell you that there's a hide tannery and wool scouring works there now.

Sheep and cattle were doing so well that the Borthwicks began treating the skins for export and preparing wool for the mills, so they set up the plant above those falls. A little ferry used to take the men over each morning but soon a few houses were built and a town grew around the mill.

I did argue about the location. I went to old man Borthwick but he just stared at me in disbelief. How could anyone not want progress in the district? Some of my own students were employed there after they left school. Borthwick's jaw was agape until a tiny gleam came into his eyes.

'How is the library going, Mrs Mathews? Short of a few books? Perhaps this can help.' He held out a £20 note. He had completely misunderstood me, but how could I convince him that I was concerned about the water, the estuary. I tried to say that the purity of the water was the most important thing, more important to my students than books, but he thought I was bargaining.

'Twenty-five pounds, Mrs Mathews and not a penny more . . . but perhaps a small plaque on the library door, Borthwick's Scouring Mill, something of that nature. Thirty pounds then and I'm sure I can get Mr Hull to add another ten or twenty.'

And to my great shame I took it. And put up the plaque. Took Hull's twenty pounds as well. That library became one of the best in the whole colony. Even today, scholars write to the school asking to view our historical monographs and maritime collection. We started a naval certificate for our boys and soon we were teaching sailors, tutoring them for their Masters' tickets. The school's future was assured, all our futures were assured.

I went back a little while later, Johnny, and you can't recognise the place. The ferns have all gone, of course, and the rocks above the falls are foul with offal and the stink of the place is putrid. Great rafts of green slime cover the creek and creep into the estuary.

Oh, the little town is pretty enough, beautiful views of the river and estuary. Beauty Point they call it now but I think of what it has replaced. That same night

I walked around George Town recalling those early evenings when I walked the streets of the town, admiring its placid prettiness, but I noticed the gutters carrying the slops and effluent from the public house straight into the river, straight across the oyster beds where we used to collect our shellfish.

Why would you do that, Johnny? Why would you not see the harm it would do, the privilege it would destroy? The privilege of being able to heedlessly drink the water and eat the mussels.

It seems to me that the human can't build a house without destroying his home. Well most humans, anyway.

Did I ever tell you about the stone houses at Sea Elephant Bay, Johnny? Those Bunurong people must have lived in them long before Caleb and the *Ocean* arrived. They were small, only big enough for seven or eight people and low roofed but they'd be comfortable. They reminded me of the houses at Skomer where I lived before Caleb came to get me. I've told you all about those poor people. All they did was tack up bits of hessian to the walls the first inhabitants had built. They would have been Celts of some kind I suppose. The people were so poor, not two pennies to rub together, not two thoughts to compare. But not just penny poor. Poor in spirit. They were outcast, desperate, insufficient imagination to invest the island and their lives with significance.

That's what the shape of the Buronong houses recalled, but I imagined how snug they would have been in this milder climate, especially inhabited with the spirit of people like your Uncle Bung Eye and Aunty Ida. Not cowed, unrefined people, but people in full possession of their law and culture.

And that culture made me think of the great library at Tamar School, the fine books, the learning, the spring of ideas . . . and to think of the pounds that purchased them. Can you have an orchestra without a rich man's purse, Johnny? Answer me that. Can you produce what our civilisation produced without theft and slavery?

Borthwick and Hull's pounds allowed us to buy some of the world's great literature. The library is known for its maritime history collection but we filled it with ideas too, dangerous things which have set one man against another, one civilisation against another.

I read them myself after you were gone. The evenings were so long. I read about the Sumerians, the Egyptians, the Greeks, the Ottomans, the Chinese, Aztecs, Russians, I read about them all, their gold, their fantastic art, the refinement of their culture, but it seemed to me the most crucial thing they shared, apart from the idea, was the slave, the labourer to illuminate someone else's idea. Someone envisages a pyramid, a slave carries the stone, someone envisages a temple of gold, a slave spends his life in a tunnel, someone designs a system of canals and someone's back is twisted by mattock and shovel. One man's glory, another man's yoke.

Someone lives in a castle and someone else lives in a pit on Skomer. Your houses were not much better, Johnny, a bit airier perhaps, fires less smoky, better climate, warmer rugs, vegetable vines growing over the turf rooves, but still just stone huts.

The big difference was that everybody had similar houses, shared the food, the labour, the celebratory dance. That's what I observed anyway and Violet told me of how she remembers growing up on the beaches around Swan Island, how the great trench ovens were swept out each morning with goose wings, new baskets woven every afternoon and fish, wallaby, possum, potato, greens, all wrapped in separate baskets and cooked under hot stones in the ovens. How the removal of food was greeted with song, how the elders dispersed the food according to the law, each with enough, each person taking food to the one they'd been designated to provide for, designated that role even before they drew their first breath.

Violet told me that with tears rolling out of her

eyes, told me that time I was ill after the wagon tipped Perc Whittaker into the pond.

No castle, no slave, no gold, no fences. Have you ever heard anything like it anywhere? They call it primitive now, denigrate the rudimentary technologies, laugh at the preparation of the food, but a civilisation without slaves, slums or ghettoes, Johnny, is that not advanced? That is what I hoped for you, that you might re-learn those things and argue your people's case, as you'd begun to do as a child. Not an easy road, not a pleasant life, but one your people require. They need you, Johnny, I need you.

I'm dying, that's why I want you to come. I want you to answer those questions for me because no one I've ever met before has ever seen the question, so how could they have the answer?

Aunty Ida says she sent a message to you with Caleb Mathews, he's working on the Kennedy boys' fishing boat. He was at the school for a while, Belle's grandson.

Just to see you would be enough, Johnny, I'm not really expecting answers.

Three
WYBALENA

Oh, you've probably heard of that, eh, Wybalena? Where the mission used to be. Where that crazy man dumped the people. You couldn't pick a more exposed part of the coast. A straight, narrow shore backed by a flat open plain. Oh, yeah good for cows, maybe, good for pigs, but people? No, people need shelter. The locks are rusted now that ignorance is preferred to a belated salvation. The mad priests gone to try the theory of evolution on a different people, a people not yet proven unworthy of divine intervention.

With God and King off their backs, the remnants of that settlement moved out of the wind to the lee of a headland sheltered by a group of bald islands off the coast. They didn't know it yet but already people were arguing about the division of that reserve amongst their white selves. No Englishman wants to live on a reserve because he knows that the word means temporary.

But the people, the Straits people didn't know that, they just knew that, for the time being, they'd been left alone. So they built their houses facing the way they wanted them to face, built them from the old stones of their prison. It wasn't much but they thought of it as their own.

A light shines golden in one of the rooms. A low room. The walls are made of stone but it's too dark to see what makes the roof. A lamp spills a buttery, tallowy light.

Wispy shreds of down float in an air almost tangibly greasy. Seven people are squatting in the room, bent over the birds they are plucking. If you could watch them for a period of time you would hear a companionable conversation, occasional laughter, the slap of naked birds in the enamel basin, rounds of songs broken by curses as one singer or another coughs on a shred of flock, you'd hear argument and derisive laughter, you'd hear the scretch of quills torn from flesh, but above all you'd smell the oil and see the slippery butter light.

The door burst open and a figure leaned in from the harsh rectangle of daylight.

'Aunty, there's a boat comin'.'

'Whose boat?'

'Chub an' Stock.'

'How long 'til they land?'

'Half an hour.'

'Alright, get Gracie to put the pots on. They'll have crayfish for us. Elly, get that boat off the jetty, they'll need all that room. Nice boat those boys 'ave got. Shut that door now, Alec, it's bloody freezin'. Did you get all them birds finished?'

'Yes, Aunt.'

'All barrelled up?'

'Yes, Aunty. Nearly.'

'Well hurry up, the Kennedys might take 'em over to Melbourne for us.' The door shut again. 'Alright, Gwennie, stop gloomin' over there. I can hardly see ya, but I can feel ya mopin' from here. I'm sendin' that Alec over to George Town an' that's that. If he ever gets a proper education he might come back and marry ya but if he doesn't there's more chicks in the rookery than ya can hit with a stick. I want him to go to Tamar, get his Master's ticket, get a boat like them Kennedys I reckon. Good school that Tamar. Good school. That poor Mrs Mathews is no good, you know, no good at all, crook down lower. Real crook. Did I ever tell you about the time she took Aunty Dilly in? When she had Johnny?'

'Yes, Aunt, yesterday.'

'Bullshit yesterday, Vronica. We wasn't even pluckin' birds yesterday.'

'Day before.'

'Bullshit.'

'Aunty, what happened to Aunty Dilly?'

'Not tellin'. You mob too snotty listen my stories. Right Vronica, know too much listen your Aunt?'

'She got killed that's all.'

'That's all, Vronica, that's all is it? Just killed? Now don't you listen to that Vronica, Bub, Aunty Dilly wasn't just killed, she was murdered. And I can tell ya when. Zackly. 1830. Fence of Legs. All them gubba come back from their big war and all they could find was our Aunty and they broke her up with clubs, that's what happened. 1830, you mark my words. Right there in Mrs Mathews' back yard. That's what happened. That's why Mrs Mathews was his mother after that, looked after him. An' that's why the Kennedy boys are bringin' a letter over from her to send up to Johnny wherever he is these days. 'Coz she's dyin' now, poor thing.'

Pluck, pluck, pluck. Pluck and butter light, oil stench and feather cloud. And silence.

'That's what happened to Aunty Dilly. That's what happened to lotta our people. Lotta our people taken on them boats in those days, knocked up by them sealer fellas an' then kicked out. Fucked up an' pregnant. Don't laugh, you Vronica, that's where you come from, don't you act toffy, your grandmother was on them boats don't you worry. Knocked her up quick smart. All you girls got that sealer in you, don't you worry, an' that bloody Gavin. Eh, Bub, give 'im a dig in the ribs will ya, wake the bludger up.'

'What, what . . .?'

'Work is what, Gav, pluckin'.'

'I'm not pluckin', Aunt, I'm crook.'

'You're crook alright, Gav, crook in the guts from the grog an' crook in the heart from bludgin' on the rest of us.'

'Not bludgin', Aunty, I'm crook I tell ya.'

'Well what about helpin' us honest people make a few pennies?'

'What honest people?'

'You heard, Mr Fancy Pants. Honest people who work for a livin' an' don't go pinchin' other people's stuff.'

'What pinchin'?'

'You heard.'

'I never, Aunt, I went fishin', got paid, that's what.'

'Not according to the Kennedy boys.'

'Fuck the Kennedy boys.'

'Yeah, too honest fa you, Gav, too willing to work for your liking, Mr Fancy Pants. Too willing to marry the girls they fuck up. Hey, what you got to say about that, eh?'

'Never fucked no one up.'

'Hear that, Bub, Mr Fancy Pants never fucked our Alice. Must 'ave been 'maculate conception, eh. Our Alice must been fucked by God. That right, Gav?'

'Ease up, Aunty.'

'No easin' up, Vronica. How's that goin' to help us. Alice with another baby, no man willin' to bend his back to work for it's food, only willin' to bend his back to cause trouble.'

'Shh, Aunty.'

'No shh, he's trouble, bringin' his lazy little guli over here an' his bag of bottles. Trouble is all.'

'Youse can all fuck off then. Ya weren't too proud to drink all me bottles, not too proud then. So yez can all fuck off. I'm goin'.'

The violent slash of light scythed the room in half, down billowed in the air from the door's sudden draft.

'Good riddance.'

'Ease up, Aunty, he's only . . . tryin' to have a bit of fun.'

'You pay for fun, Vronica, you pay, you mark my words, you pay, or you go around like Mr Fancy Pants, fuckin' up other people's lives. Anyway, 'bout time we cleaned up an' went to meet the boys. There's two fellas know how to show bit a respect.'

'Not just respect they show either, Aunt!'

'Well, they pay. Whatever they do, they pay. When they have fun they pay. Don't worry 'bout that. You could do worse than that, Vronica.'

'I have.'

'Alright, alright, what's past is past. Let's get down to the jetty. It's that bludger Gavin gets on my wick. No need for us to fight and mope, just because some man don't know how to make his bed.'

And the Kennedy boys did bring a crayfish and they did bring a cask of beer from Boags and they did agree to take the mutton bird oil to Melbourne, just like they agreed to try and get a letter to Johnny Mullagh up on the Murray.

You shouldn't need to know who I am, but I know your type, you won't let it rest until you find out, so, just let it be said that I'm Yolla, Moonbird, spirit of all the plucked mutton birds. These islands are death islands see. Been like that for fifty years and now all my little chickens are killed for the same reason that all them Palewa were killed here. Greed. Money. And when you live like that the spirits of the dead are all around you, you hear their cries, even when you don't know what it is that's flutterin' in your heart, wakin' you up. It's wings, wings of all them dead birds.

So just let's say I'm Yolla an' I see everythin' an' just

let's say that Aunty Ida is my wife. She don't know it, just like there's a lot she don't know about her people, but just let's say I'm Yolla and she my wife. That why she says things she don't even know she know. Surprises even herself. But she knows it comes from someplace. Off the sea. Wings off the sea. That's Aunty Ida, knowin' without knowin'.

That her bed husband down there, Uncle Georgie Hummock. Hardly says nothin' that Uncle Georgie. Lot of the kids can't understand a word he says. Talkin' language most of the time. Talkin' it 'isself that why. He's been able to explain a few things to Aunty Ida because there's four proofs of his persuasiveness but most of the time he just shuts up.

Oh, he's part of it alright. Doesn't stop him bein' part of it, doesn't stop him makin' sure the fish is cooked right and the beer barrel is cooled down in the well and it doesn't mean it stops him talkin' his lingo and usin' my name all the time. Moonbird! He's the Moonbird. Look at him, sittin' by the fire roastin' them birds on a bit of fencin' wire with all them kids and dogs racin' 'round, gone mad with the excitement of the lollies them Kennedy boys brought over from Tassie.

Aunty Ida still calls it Van Diemen but the boys call it Tassie, everyone says Tasmania now, pretend they don't know what you're talkin' about when you say Van Diemen.

Anyway, everyone's all got 'emselves in a tiz because of the visitors. Visitors are always welcome on the island, especially the Kennedys, not just coz of the presents they bring, not just because they're family, but they're good lookin' boys an' all the women get 'emselves a bit excitable, like the kids with the lollies.

So there's Uncle Georgie friggin' around with his fencin' wire toastin' fork, Vronica has got the kero tin boilin' good an' proper for the crays an' makin' sure the boys get a good look at her tits while she's at it. They're married now, but there's no harm in tryin' is Vronica's theory. There's six dogs, seven, no eight, the bitch is under the tankstand with the pups an' there's twelve kids chasin' 'em, thirteen if ya count Gavin, who's tryin' to get back in everybody's good books, which will last him as long as the cask has still got beer. Caleb Mathews is there, too, Belle's grandson, he's goin' over to Melbourne on the Kennedy's boat. *Yolla* they called her, *Yolla*, see, reckon they know everythin' those boys, but it's respectful I suppose. Gwennie and Bubby are slicin' up vegetables and Aunty Ida is pokin' at the mussels and oysters tryin' to keep the kids and dogs from kickin' ash in 'em.

'Get out of it, you dogs,' she yells, 'Gwennie, kick that Gavin up the arse. Billy, careful of Uncle George there. *Billy*, watch what ya doin'.'

The Kennedy boys have tapped the cask an' everyone gets a cupful. Gavin gets two of course. Hides one on the tankstand behind the geranium, but the bitch gets that. Them pups make ya thirsty as hell. Wallert they call the bitch. Anyway, she feels a lot better after Gav's cup of beer an' she sidles over to Uncle George draggin' her dugs in the sand, squirmin' up beside him, slidin' her snout under the old man's hand.

'Oh, garl,' he mutters, 'you bil woori garl.'

'What you sayin', Uncle?' Chubber Kennedy asks, polite enough, but Uncle pretends he doesn't hear and keeps on murmurin' to the dog, slidin' his hand over her head, feelin' the tits for the mastitis an' fever an' such, rubbin' his thumb along her spine. The bitch closes her eyes an' her little pink tongue slips a tip between her lips, oh she loves that Uncle George, loves him talkin' to her.

'Woori garl, woori garl, wernen dilp dalang, eh? Wate nubiyt, wate bobup, wate longa cora. Bilma kunyaba woori garl, eh. Bilma kunyaba nganya goork. Kunyaba nganya goork.'

'What's Uncle sayin', Aunty?' Chubber Kennedy asked.

'Oh he talkin' his lingo to hisself.'

'I can't understand a word he's sayin'.'

'Well that's the way he likes it, that fella. Just the way he likes it. He not from here you know.'

'Come over with Captain Scott from Victoria didn't he?'

'That was later. First time was with that Aunty Trugannini. Got the blame for killin' those white men. That's how he got here. True name Woollert Putcha.'

'What's that Aunt?'

'Fat possum or somethin'. Think he'd ever tell ya somethin' like that? Can't get a word out of him 'bout that time, all those years on Maria an' then out here watchin' the ol' people die on this place. Old Fat Possum. That dog hears more about that time than us people. Know what he calls her? Wallert. He calls her his possum rug or some such thing. Don't expect me to know what he's talkin' 'bout all the time. I thought I was his possum rug, but these days it's that dog he tells his secrets to.'

Aunty Ida scraped the mussels out of the fire and flicked specks of ash off their shells with a blade of rush grass, fussing to get the plate to the table while they were still hot, the juice still simmering in the shells.

Chubber took one, passing it twitchily from hand to hand trying not to burn himself.

'Oh good, Aunty, them mussels is beautiful.' He sucked the juice out of the shell, chucked it on the fire and went to sit where he could hear Uncle talking to the dog, shamelessly feeling her tits between his fingers, the dog on its back, eyes closed, bottom lip stretched taut in ecstasy.

'Oh, warrawan baab nanyaki Wallert, ooh warrawan, warrawan, bobup bitjarra, eh, ooh warrawan, warrawan.'

'Here, you ol' possum,' Aunty Ida came over and held out some mussels to the old man and he sucked them out of the shell without speaking before turning back and murmuring his warrawan litany to the bitch.

'Can't help himself, poor ol' fella. He's Bunurong, you know. That's what his mob is. And he thinks he's goin' back there, that's what I reckon, thinks he's goin' back to his country, slippin' away from us back to his own place.'

'I could take him over, Aunty.'

'That fella won't need a boat, Chubber, you wait an' see. Next Moonbird flight, I reckon. He's been talkin' to them birds too, you know, tellin' them he's sorry. I know that much of his lingo. That's why he won't never eat them birds, won't even look at 'em. Easy to get out of the pluckin' if you ask me. Don't look at me like that Chub, I know he's not a bad fella, but how am I supposed to feel. It's terrible to kill all them birds, but you tell me how I'm supposed to feed all this mob. Yabberin' to a dog's not goin' to help, whisperin' to Yolla not goin' to help. It's food in bellies, that what I'm stuck with.'

'Aunty, I've gotta talk to you about a coupla things. Them church people on the mainland are goin' around collectin' all the pale kids an' stickin' 'em in a home down in Hobart. Guvman's passed this law says they can. For their own good they say.'

'For their own good!'

'Yeah, well that's what they say. Sometimes offer the young girls money for their babies, tell 'em they'll get good schoolin' an' such like. And Aunty, some of them girls take the money.'

'Some of 'em would.'

'But when they sober up they change their minds an' it's too late.'

'Bloody grog.'

'Not just grog, Aunty, some of them girls don't care.'

'Well some is not all, Chub. Sure those girls should get off their arse but I heard from George Town they're takin' kids while their mothers is workin'.'

'That's right, Aunty. They got little Archie Boag like that. Fanny nearly went mad. Won't even let her visit him. Says it's unsettlin'.'

'Unsettlin'! Course it's unsettlin' seein' the mother what loves him.'

'Anyway, Aunt, I come and told ya because they've been takin' kids off the islands. Even down on Tasman, took Nugget's two little girls, you know, works on the lighthouse down on Swan Island.'

'Nugget? What they take his kids for?'

'Like I was sayin', Aunt.'

'But Doris an' him 'ave always looked after those girls. Only last Christmas, no Christmas before, I seen 'em down at George Town, down . . . They can't do that.'

'Just keep your eyes open, Aunty.'

'Mutjaka, nganya goork, kulkurn guli, yani yu, kurrman, yani yu gurrk.'

'What's Uncle sayin', Aunty?'

'Oh, I dunno, Chub, somethin' about goin' away with the seals. Reckon he's away with the pixies.'

'Yani yu, yani yu, plurry bagurk, yani yu, kurrman.' The old man flung his arm out to the east and glared at Aunty Ida.

'Well speak English then, Fat Old Possum, how we supposed to understand?'

'Buggery bitch, plurry buggery, mutjaka kulkurn guli, mutjaka nganya goork, yani yu gurrk.'

'Alright, alright, over to Seal Island and teach 'em things, you know, teach about . . .'

'Initiation, Aunt?'

'Oh well, you know what he's like, Chub.'

'Well why not, why not take 'em over there? Get 'em out of the way for a while. They'll never find you over there.'

'But how long would we have to be there for? I don't wanna leave my house. Why should I?'

'For the kids, Aunt. Just for a little while. Me an' Stock will bring ya stuff every few weeks.'

'Where'll we sleep?'

'We'll fix something up.'

'Wurrung, kumba wurrung.'

'What's he say, Aunt?'

'Sleep in bloody blackfellas' house, he says. Alright

fa you, ol' Possum, but I'm a lady, I don't sleep with bloody spiders an' snakes.'

Uncle George shrugged his shoulders and began murmuring to his dog who was squirming beside his legs, trying to get her head underneath his hand again, jealous that he'd been distracted.

'Oh, woori garl, kunyaba woori garl, oh kunyaba nganyaki woori garl.'

'I don't wanna go all the way over there. What about my big girls? How they goin' to get on?'

'They'll be right, Aunt, they're big enough to look after themselves.'

But Aunty sulked and drank several cups of the blackest sweetest tea she could make.

'Bilma merrijee, bagurk.'

'Good, you reckon? That's what you think, Old Possum, it'll be bloody cold, that's what.'

'Youdorro, youdorro wurrung, plenny weing, plenny kutja.'

'I'm too old for all that, Poss, me bones ache. I don't care how much food there is.'

'Aunty?'

'What you wan', Vronica?'

'I'll look after them girls, I've been talkin' to Chub about it.'

'Been talkin' with your tits far as I can see.'

'Oh, ease up, Aunt, me an' Chub got an arrange-ment.'

'"rangement, pah.'

'Well don't listen, Aunty, but if we lose the kids then no one's goin' to thank you.'

'I'm too old for wanderin' all over the bloody Strait.'

'It's five miles, Aunty. Five miles.'

'No stove, no bloody chairs, where's an old lady gunna sit?'

'Mum burre.'

'Sit on your own mum, Possum, you find a soft rock, an' you sit down on yer mum. Ladies need a chair.'

'You no lady, Aunty, you're a mutton bird plucker.'

'And you're a married man fucker.'

'Am not.'

'Well, what you doin' shimmyin' roun' that Chub for?'

'My business is my business, Aunty.'

'Oh, Vronica, I'm too old for gallivantin'. I don't wanna be rude, bub, but look, you've always been me favourite niece ya know that, don't ya?'

'Yes, Aunt.' Veronica must have been waiting to hear something of the kind and went and sat next to her aunt, pressed right up against her beefy arm, not exactly like Wallert squirming beneath Uncle George's hand but bloody close.

'Don't cry now, Aunty.'

'Oh, Vronica, I'm gettin' old, an' all I want is peace. I want all our people just to have bit of peace. I want that Alec to get a boat like Chub and Stock, make somethin' of himself. Don't let Gwennie do somethin' stupid, Vronica, make her wait until Alec's got himself set up.'

'Too late, Aunty, I think it's a bit late.'

'Oh, Vronica, Vronica, why can't those bloody men keep their guli to 'emselves?'

'Because we won't let 'em, Aunt.'

'Vronica, what about you? You're smart, you're good lookin'. What are you goin' ta do? Be a bloody plucker with a handful of bastard kids?'

'No, Aunt.'

'Well what, then. Seein' Chub every three months? What about his wife an' kids?'

'There's no wife.'

'There was.'

'Not now there's not.'

'What about the kids then, more bloody bait for that church mob.'

'The kids is comin' over here.'

'More kids. Not even married, Vronica and you gunna 'ave three kids.'

'Could be five for all I care. I love him, Aunty. Always have.'

'Well that's all very fine, but does he love you?'

'Seems so.'

'Is he listenin' to us? Can he hear or does he know? He's bringin' that bloody crayfish over here.'

'Aunty, I've brought the cray tail for you.'

'I don't like crayfish.'

'Oh, Aunty, 'course you do, you love them crayfish me an' Stock bring over.'

'Not anymore.'

'She's in a pisser, Chub, because of you bringin' your kids over here. Reckons you don't love me. That's what she says.'

''Course I love her, Aunt.'

'Since when?'

'Since the picnic races at Preservation.'

'You was eight.'

'Since I was eight.'

'You don't love someone at eight. You don't want to slave your guts out makin' sure they've got enough to eat. You don't leave your wife to chase after another woman at eight.'

'She's not my wife, Aunt.'

'What then?'

'Look Aunty, that's my business, but I'm tellin' you the truth.'

'Gunna marry this one then?'

''Course.'

'Or just dump your kids?'

'Aunty, do you reckon I'd do that? You're talkin' to Chubber, Aunty, I'm the fat boring one remember, I'm the one who washed his own shirts, looked after his sisters. Don't you remember, Aunty?'

'Kiss her then.'

'What?'

'Kiss her.'

'Alright.'

'Not like that. Kiss her proper. Alright, that'll do.

Youse two can stop that now. Everyone's lookin'. You'll be the talk of the islands by tomorrow. That's enough, alright. Now look, Vronica, if I'm going over to that lump of rock with all them kids then you an' Gwennie is comin' too. An' I want that Gavin somewhere else. Can he fish with you an' Stock, Chub?'

'No, Aunt, he's bloody hopeless, he's dangerous on a ship. That's somethin' I won't do. He's bad luck, I can't have that on board *Yolla*. Stock wouldn't have it either.'

'Well Alec will have to stay back for a bit. We'll take Bubby and Gwennie with us. Alec will have to keep Gavin under control. If he can.'

'Woori garl, too.'

'Oh, that right, Possum, we're shufflin' the deck to keep the family on an' even keel an' all you can think about is takin' ol' flea bag. That'd be right. Thanks a lot, Possum, thanks fa bein' the man of the island. Like bein' married to Napoleon.'

'Who's Napolean, Aunt?'

'Fisherman on King Island.' At least Aunty Ida had enough remaining good humour to wink at her niece.

Veronica thought it was only five miles away, but she didn't know her arse from her elbow. Uncle George's Seal Island was on the other side of the strait but Veronica was prepared to say anything to get a ride on Chub's boat. And not just his boat.

It can be an ugly passage, especially when you punch into the westerly the whole way. Aunty Ida went green and spent the journey with her face on the gunnel hoping for a big wave to sweep her away. Uncle George sat up in the bow with his dog, muttering and murmuring as he stroked her head. Alec kept one of the female pups, which he called Nganya, Bubby brought one which she called Gavin because it shit itself all the time, and don't ask what happened to the rest.

On about the evening of the second day, Aunty Ida

thought it was her last, they passed the first piece of land since leaving home, a small almost naked bulb of rock with a rough stone lighthouse. There were about six lights in the strait by this time and this was the most recent. It looked shithouse.

'Deal Island,' Stock said, pointing at it. That passed for conversation from Stock.

'Murnnatja,' said Uncle George and that passed for conversation from him.

'Old Galub Mathews is the keeper,' Chubber said to Aunty Ida.

She vomited over the side and for the time being that passed for conversation from her.

'Aren't you scared he'll see all of us blackfellas, Chub?' Veronica asked.

'Nup, he's blind, poor old bloke.'

Sometimes Caleb could tell when a boat was passing because of the way the gulls changed their shrieks to a . . . well, a different kind of shriek. But apart from keeping the whale oil up to the light and washing the windows he didn't bother too much about passing traffic because he couldn't wait to get back to his journal where he sought to explain himself to himself. And the gulls didn't seem to mind him. A man without most of his face was destined to become gull scraps soon enough, anyway.

'Kurrman,' said Uncle George, as they approached another island at dawn the next day.

'Sea Elephant,' said Stock who liked to get things right.

The old cannon was still on the point but the sheds on the jetty were just a jumble of timber. Caleb and Eugenie's cabin was still there although the door was off its hinges and penguins thought it was good-o under the floorboards, but penguins are like that. The men's hut had been burnt and the roof was a snare of blackened rafters.

'We can stick a sail cloth over that,' said Chubber, calculating.

Aunty Ida sat up and stared at the Captain's hut and wondered if there could still be a chair left inside . . . and a stove.

Uncle George threw the bitch into the water before they tied up and swam with her to the beach.

'Where you goin'?' the old lady yelled, a little recovered now that death had been postponed.

'Wurrung.'

'Wurrung, you stupid old bastard, what about givin' us a hand here. To your wife.'

But Uncle George simply stepped onto the sand and marched off over the rise with his dog.

'Well he's going to be a big help. Like a cup of tea, dear? Another bit of cake, my sweetykins?'

Veronica and Chubber laughed, Stock wondered how long before he could get back to sea, Bubby wondered if the pup could swim if she chucked it in to wash the shit off it, the kids cast their gaze over the desolate village of hut and burnt out shed and wondered where the food was kept.

Stock didn't even step ashore, never even pulled the sail down completely, just tied *Yolla* up loose and waited to get back to sea.

Chubber helped them get ashore as best they could, as best as you can when you can hear the sails on your boat slapping fretfully at the boom. That bloody Stock.

Aunty Ida sniffed about Captain Mathews' cabin, slapped a cloth across the table, poked her nose in the tea canister, nothing, and tried out the chairs as Chubber slammed a few four inch nails into the hinges to get the door back on.

'Good as gold, Aunty,' he declared.

'Gold, ya reckon. Hmmph.'

'And Vronica will make sure you're looked after, Aunt.'

'And who's gunna look after Vronica, Chub?'

'Me. I told ya, Aunt. Have I ever not done what I said?'

'Is it what you want, Chub? It's no good if you

don't want it that way. Not a man like you, wanderin' around the ports. It wouldn't work.'

'Aunt, one of these days they're gunna stop chasin' us people around.'

'You reckon?'

'And when they do I'm gunna build a house on the island, not far from yours maybe, and that's where me an' Vronica and the kids are gunna live.'

'And you two'll be happy to be mutton bird pluckers?'

'Won't be pluckin' birds, Aunt. Me an' Stock'll keep fishin' the crays an' the couta. Made an arrangement with George Town to send fish an' crays to Hobart. Big place that Hobart, Aunt.'

'You've been doin' a lot of thinkin', Chub.'

'Get a lot of time out at sea, Aunt. But anyway I'm gunna take young Caleb over to the mainland to see if he can get that message up to Johnny Mullagh an' buy a few things an' then I'll go back to the island an' see if that church mob have been snoopin' around, see if Gavin hasn't burnt it to the ground.' He looked about the hut, impatient to go. 'This was old Galub Mathews' place, Aunt.'

'And Eugenie. This was her cup by the looks.'

'Sad how that all went bust.'

'Oh well, there was a lot of bad seed sown into these winds, Chub.'

'Too right, Aunt. Anyway look, here comes Vronica and the kids with all your things. Tea an' sugar an' flour.'

'Won't be any milk, but.'

'That's why we brought the goat, Aunty.'

'Don't like goats. Remind me of that George.' But all the kids burst in and began to unwrap stuff they had no right to unwrap, hopin' to find biscuits or something.

Chubber kissed Veronica quickly, believing that nobody noticed, and then strode off down to the jetty.

Veronica busied herself with putting away the foodstuffs and clearing away the swallows' nest from the top of the cupboards.

'This is old Mrs Mathews first house in Australia, you know. Came out on the *Ocean* with Captain Mathews, as a bride. But it never worked out. Not often does with sailors.'

'Alright, Aunt.'

'Is it? You don't even know what happened to them people. How do you know it's alright.'

'Me an' Chub will do better than that.' Little Gracie and Gwennie rolled their eyes at each other while stuffing their faces with their aunt's biscuits.

'Get outa them biscuits, you girls. They're me medicinals. You outa know better, Gwennie, 'specially with a name like yours.'

'What do you mean, Aunt?'

'You know how you got your name?'

'Yeah, Queenie, everyone knows that.'

'Yes, but where does Queenie come from, eh?'

'Queen of England, I suppose.'

'No, smarty pants, Queen of Tasmania, Queenie Trugannini. That why you should start actin' your age. You ask Uncle George.'

'Where is Uncle George?'

'Oh he's gone over to the old people's houses up on the point. He'll be moonin' around up there with that blasted dog. Dunno why we come to this place at all. There was trouble here, you know. All them sailors, even that Captain Mathews so I was told, all of 'em treatin' our people bad.'

'That Bunurong mob killed some of Captain Mathews men was what I was told, Aunty.'

''Course they did, Vronica, had to after they treated our women like that. Law. Had to. Rapin' 'em, beltin' 'em up. Terrible they were. Our mob kill a coupla poxy sailors an' all hell breaks loose.'

The kids could feel a story comin' on and slowly trickled away. Except Errol, the one with the bung leg, who found it hard to trickle, and besides, he loved stories.

'What ol' Captain Scott told Uncle George, was that

there was a lot of trouble here, an' then that old Galub went down to our islands where some of them were hidin' an' he came on Aunty Belle an' he goes to grab her an' the warriors start chuckin' spears an' he shoots 'em. And then he brings Belle back over here. Does his business on the way. Dumps her over there at Port Albert an' comes back to Seal Elephant. Here. But he's got the clap 'coz them sealers give it to Belle and she gives it to him, if he didn't already have it, and he gives it to that Eugenie who looked like it was a miracle she could ever get it.'

'Aunty!'

'Well she's such a sourpuss at times.'

'She's been good to a lot of our people, Aunt.'

'Too right she has, Vronica, that's not what I'm sayin'. I'm sayin' she don't dance naked on the beach at midnight.'

'Who you talkin' 'bout, Aunt?'

'You, Vronica, think no one seen ya?'

'Wasn't naked.'

'Bloody close.'

'He asked me to marry him.'

'Just as well. But sailors is hard husbands, Vronica, almost worse than them ol' possums.'

'You done alright, Aunt.'

'Oh, I done alright, I'm not sayin' that but I'm just warnin' ya it's not all dancin' on the beach with ya tits out.'

'Did not, Aunt.'

'Not what Gwennie said.'

'She's just jealous 'coz Professor Alec can't dance.'

'Not what I've heard. Not by the look of Gwennie's belly. Anyway, I'm just warnin' ya, because nothin' causes more trouble than bad blood between a man an' a woman. Look at that Eugenie over there, dyin' alone, not even a child to look out for her, has to go beggin' someone else's kid to kiss her coffin.'

'And old Captain Mathews out there on Deal Island.'

'That what they call it these days. Alone in his bloody stone tower is what I call it.'

'And blind, Chub said.'

'See what I mean. No good, everythin' turns bad when a man an' a woman go against each other.'

'Aunty, why's he out there on his own if he's blind?'

'Well, Errol, I reckon it's the spirits. He let the spirits in. He loved that Belle, you know. That's what Aunty Fanny always said. Couldn't take his eyes off her. Not like most men look at women, but . . . a bit like Chub looks at Vronica, I suppose.'

'Oh, Aunt.'

'True.'

'Did Uncle George look at you like that, Aunty?'

'Errol, you ever seen Uncle George look direct at anyone? That man looks past ya, always has done, like he's lookin' over the edge of the world, always lookin' out over the edge. Always like that. I was scared stiff when I was younger. 'Til I found out he was just a man. Just a man, he was, but in his head, Errol, is stuff that . . . well, my boy, when you're a bit older maybe . . .'

'He might tell me about the edge of the world?'

'He might, if he stops talkin' to that dog long enough.'

'Tell us about Captain Mathews and Aunty Belle.'

'Well, Vronica, far as I can tell from what Aunty Fanny said he really loved her. Even before he married Mrs Mathews an' his men had Granny Woonaji an' Belle an' Fanny over here, Captain Mathews used to hang around while they fished in the bay. Used to ask all about us peoples, you know. Aunty Fanny reckons he couldn't take his eyes off Belle even then, an' so when he saw her down there on our islands he sort of went to pieces.'

'And what happened to Aunty Belle?'

'Well she was pregnant with young Caleb by then, but sick with the sealers' disease and she got tied up in

that business with Trugannini and Uncle George and
that's how she come back to our islands I think.
Couldn't stay over at Port Albert because after they
killed those two sailors, the police was shootin' any
black person they seen. Even though the sailors was
stealin' women. They was off the *Ocean* so they say.
Sailors off the *Ocean* lookin' for women and then there
was murder everywhere. Uncle George said all the
camps was empty by the time they took him over to
Maria Island. Anyway Aunty Belle died almost as soon
as Caleb was born. She called him Caleb after his father.
Caleb Mathews. Everyone knew who his father was.
Eugenie musta known too.

'I always liked that woman, you know. Never seen
her all that often but whenever she looked at me, an' it
wasn't just me, any of our peoples, she saw you, remembered your name even. Captain Scott was like that, too.
Them two shoulda got together, you know. I don't like
to see good people lonely. Some people don't need other
people, you know, remember that ol' Bungey, he was
like that, but he was brought up for that, made like that,
law man, that what ol' Bungey was. Had to be movin'
'bout here, goin' over there, keepin' an eye on things,
it'd be like lovin' an albatross, see it once every two
years, or such.'

'Tell us the story about Aunt Woonaji, Aunt.' Errol
asked, keen to keep the stories coming. It's hard to say if
it was the crook leg that made Errol more interested in
listening to the stories of his grandparents and uncles
and aunts or whether he would have just been like that
anyway. A thoughtful kid. A listener. And listeners
become story tellers in their time.

'Aunty Woonaji?'

'And old Mr West.'

'Who you been talkin' to?'

'Uncle George.'

'Yeah, that'd be right. Well I've never seen Aunty
Woonaji since when I was a real little pupup an' I never
seen that Mr West at all. Some people say he dead, she

dead, an' then ya hear someone went over to Barren an' bought a load of fish off the ol' lady, never see the ol' fella at all, that's why the story goes he dead, but Chub reckons Aunty Woonaji would 'ave told us, would have wanted ol' Bungey to come over an' smoke an' so forth. Chub reckons they're both still over there. Seen their fires an' their fish traps. Seen that ol' longboat on the beach. Bungey saw 'em plenny times. So Stock says. Says there's other mob there, too, wild mob. Warrigal. Could be just gammin.'

'Might be true, Aunt.'

'Mebe. All these stories, all these people runnin' aroun' hidin' from shadows like that poor Mrs Mathews. I always felt sorry for that Mrs Mathews, always felt she needed someone close to her, that why she looked after our Johnny, you know. But she needed more than that. She had a big sore in 'er guts, that woman. Big empty place. I could feel it whenever I saw her, feel it now, hurts me just thinkin' 'bout it.

'This water tastes funny, Vronica. Better look in that tank, I reckon, bet there's a bloody possum in it or somethin', them bloody possums, not much good fa nuthin'. Make the tea taste funny.'

'Could be the teapot, Aunt.'

'Na, it's the water.'

'Hey look here, Aunty, look what I found.' Errol held up the desiccated mouse newly plumped by good hot tea. 'Not the water at all, Aunt, it's a mouse.'

'That no mouse, Errol, that geram, that pigmy possum. What I said, possum in water. See, I knew that all along. You go out an' bury that animal, Errol, you bury him good, that spirit fella, he's a bit like that ol' Bungey, snoopin' about keepin' his eyes on things. You show respect that fella.'

'I'll wash out the teapot, Aunt, an' I'll make you a fresh one.'

'Chuck that teapot out, Vronica, no good that fella dyin' in there, an' I wish I hadn't sipped that bloody tea neither. Did I ever tell ya, Vronica, about them ducks?'

'Ducks, Aunty, you've got a lotta stories 'bout ducks.'

'No, no, these was Mrs Mathews ducks. At the school. Violet told us about it.'

'Here's your cuppa, Aunt.'

'Thanks, Vronica. Not bad, don't taste like mouse at any rate. You bury that geram, Errol?'

'Yes, Aunt.'

'Alright then, there was these ducks see, about twenty of 'em, Campbell's, Indian Runners, bloody Mallards, wild ducks, all sorts, on this big pond behind the school, lake really, anyway the tigers was always getting' 'em an' it was about the time when Johnny Mullagh had to leave an' the white people in town wouldn't sell Mrs Kennedy nothin'. It blew over later on when things went bust, they wasn't too proud to sell things to her then, but this was about the trouble times and so they had this scheme to get the ducks in a pen an' make 'em lay eggs, you know, sort of civilised, not just drop 'em anywhere, sit under some old cart or up in a bloody tree where no one could get 'em. It was so they could get the eggs an' a bit of roast duck an' so forth. Mrs Mathews wasn't what you'd call a farmer's wife.

'Anyways, they decide to do it blackfella way. So they got a few of the kids, blackens and whitens, ta go down the end of the lake an' beat the rushes with branches, an' the women, Violet an' a few cousins, would get in the water with bunches of weed on their head an' try an' look like a bit of swamp, ya know, like Alec does on the island. Won't use a gun, that man. Spends too much time with Uncle George if you ask me. Anyway, Mrs Mathews is sittin' on the back verandah watchin' all this, waitin' to see how it'll go like. So the kids go whack, whack, whack with their sticks an' the ducks go quack, quack, quack an' start swimmin' down toward the women. Everythin's goin' just right, but someone forgot about them two blue cattle dogs they had, an' they must 'ave got too excited, what with all the noise an' so forth, an' they comes barrellin' out from under the school just as Perc Whittaker come in the yard with 'is horse and cart. Was gunna buy some of the ducks or just sit aroun' gawkin' at the women, who knows, he was always a bit queer that Whittaker, anyway the blue dogs ran straight under the horse on their way to attack whatever they could find makin' the hullabaloo at the pond, but Whittaker's bay horse stood up on its hind legs and then took off but the harness broke and tripped up the near side horse an' it goes a cropper an' pulls the other horse with it, they're still draggin' the cart along, the horse on the ground is lashin' out with its legs and hoofs kickin' the other horse up its mum an' orf it goes an' straight in the pond, the cart stands up on its tackle poles and goes arse over ears inta the pond as well, Perc an' all. Well the dogs is off long ago, the kids are at one end of the pond, standin' with their mouths open, an' the women is tryin' to protect 'emselves from horses legs and Whittakers clawin' hands at the other, the dogs jump in to bite the horses an' the horses try to bite the dogs.

'Violet reckons it took ages to get everyone out of the pond, but they forgot about Whittaker who sank like a stone. Well it woulda been nice to leave him in there, but Violet couldn't do it so she felt around with her feet an' found him and dragged him out covered in weed an' kunang an' there was a yabby already startin' in on his nose. Ya wouldn't read about it. Anyway just as well the women was wet because they was pissin' 'emselves.

'But when things calmed down they sort of look up to see what Mrs Mathews would say about all the mess an' she's just sittin' there with her face in her hands rockin' back and forwards, back an' forwards. So Violet comes up to her, an' tears are streamin' out of her eyes, but Violet, wet as a shag as ya can imagine, can't tell whether she's laughin' or really cryin'. All she can say is, "I never . . . I never . . ." Couldn't seem to get the rest of it out. Violet didn't know what to do, but Mrs Mathews kept on cryin' and rockin', so Violet lifted her up an' put her in her bed, made her a cuppa tea an' so forth, but she was still cryin'. Violet sat up all night an' it took hours for the sobs to kinda stop.

'Next mornin' she said nuthin'. Never mentioned it at all an' Violet always reckons it was kinda hysteria, but not from laughin', but from cryin'. Like I said, the few times I seen her it was as if she was holdin' her hands over a big hole in her. I always worried about her after that.

'They never seen them ducks again neither. Or Whittaker.'

'What happened to Mr Whittaker's horse, Aunt?'

'Died, Errol, died 'a old age or shock maybe, delayed shock.'

'What about them blue dogs?'

'Oh, them dogs, they just did what blue dogs do. Eat, shit, sleep under the table and fart. Bit like Gavin, I suppose. But no matter how ya look at it them ducks is gone.'

The old lady was disgruntled by the dislocation to her life but she wasn't dismayed. There was no real teapot, thanks to the geram, so she just got on with it, but troubled, like a woman is troubled, scheming and planning so that all within range of the warmth of her gaze would be safe and well . . . and happy, even people like Mrs Mathews, who she hardly knew.

So patterns began to arrange themselves around Aunty Ida's domestic routine, and some of them even drew Uncle George within the circle.

They'd walk over the dunes and along the cliffs to the remains of the stone huts where the old fella had set up camp with his dog.

'Look at him,' Aunty Ida said when she first saw his camp. 'Reckons nothin's happened since Cook.'

'He don't think that, Aunt,' Veronica cautioned.

'I know, dear, but look at him, lyin' down on his possum skin in front of the fire an' that dog curled up at the back of his legs. Fire goin'. You know what I mean. Like nothin's changed.'

The bitch was eyeing them over the old man's legs, she knew who they were, but she'd still be growling a warning, although the old man wouldn't bother to turn around to look, be a bit ordinary to do that don't ya reckon. No, he just got straight on with his dreaming while the mob settled 'emselves down on the grass mats on the sand. Aunty Ida was asleep inside five minutes while little Gracie used her lumpy form as the hills and valleys for the adventures of the wooden doll Stock had made for her out of a bit of mahogany so dark it was almost black. Veronica built a new fire to make a cuppa, you wouldn't dare disturb the sticks of Uncle's fire, and then she joined the other women and kids checking the fish traps Uncle George had repaired. Soon the smudge of wood smoke lifted gently from the fire and you could smell the skin of fish charring and the unmistakable smell of Aunty Ida's tea steaming in the billy.

Captain Scott got them a chest of this pitch black China tea. There were still boats calling into Kowloon and Shanghai, still bringing back chests of tea and preserved ginger in jars, trading them for the smoked moon birds of Bass's Strait. Intercontinental trade relations I suppose you'd call it, with Yolla, as usual, right in the middle.

But this is what I see as I skim past that beach, an old man curled on a possum rug with a dog pressed into the crook behind his knees, a fire of four sticks and a squiggle of smoke before them. A big woman some way off on a grass mat with a little girl using her body as the world. A younger woman checking a couple of babies bundled in possum rugs, sound asleep, their milky mouths puffing sweet-breath. And several other women and a boy with a bung leg taking mullet and garfish from the fish traps while another girl readies the cooking fire.

That what I want you to see, the people on the beach going about their life, not that their breath doesn't stink and their shit doesn't smell, not that they never speak a cross word, never bear a grudge, but just that they are there, being a family, sustaining themselves from the land just like anyone else. Not saints, not sinners, people.

That's what Yolla sees, that's what Yolla does. And when old ladies sleep on the sand, in the sun, the voices of children lilting about them, they often dream. And dreams as you know can be restful or disturbing and often have nothing to do with your present circumstance.

Aunty Ida dreamt of two ravens stealing the eye from a young buck wallaby.

Sure enough, back on the home island there's trouble. Gavin and Alec fixed the roof on the plucking shed, made a dozen cray pots from tea-tree canes, repaired the bream net, got on with it generally. The brothers could work together alright but not forever.

A fisherman visited the island, braved the shoals and sandbars of the Sound after the transom of his ketch was breached, and he put in to shore to repair the timbers. Alec had seen Chub and Stock doing minor repairs on *Yolla*, so he boiled up pitch and made caulking wool out of tea-tree bark and soon the *Prion* was ready to head out through the passage. The skipper, Captain Bowman, tried to give the brothers fish but they had plenty of that, they tried to give him mutton birds but he couldn't stomach them so eventually he left Gavin with four bottles of whisky. Alec tried to refuse but Gavin was quick to allow Bowman to pay his debt and head back out to sea.

Alec knew that work was finished until the bottles were empty and so he lit a fire in the plucking shed, lit the smudgy oil lamps and set to work copying out the journal Bowman had lent him, the journal which had in fact saved Bowman's life, allowing him to negotiate the treacherous Sound that ships avoided like seals try to avoid a shark's teeth.

Alec could hear Gavin's merriment turn to song and onwards to glowering silence. For two days he kept himself to the plucking shed, absorbed in the details of the journal which he saw as a perfect introduction to the Captain's Certificate at Mrs Mathews' school.

A narrative of a Voyage to New Holland and Van Diemen's Land. Amaso Delano 1805 . . . *If necessary to make a harbour in passing the Straits, the only one I know is not safe for a ship to enter larger than two hundred tons, and when at anchor there, she is unsafe unless provided with extraordinarily good cables and anchors. When going into this harbour you will observe a number of islets to the westward of Cape Barren Island; all of them should be left to the northward of you. Some of the islets to the westward of Cape Barren are a number of miles long; but none of them so large as Preservation. The northerly passage runs up nearly east, whilst the southerly one between Clark's and Preservation is south-east. Preservation Island is low land and Clark's is higher, but by no means so high as Cape Barren. There is a number of considerable high mountains on the latter, which on approaching towards the westerly point, are discovered to make to the westward and terminate in a kind of cape, consisting of very irregular, rocky, and broken kind of land, off which lie several rocks, and ledges, one or two of which should be left on the starboard hand, on passing to the south point. If desirous to anchor, it is requisite to haul in to the southward and approach it so near as to make the passage at the entrance appear to be nearly closed up, then anchor may be cast in either nine, eight or seven fathoms.*

The latitude of Kent's Bay is 40° 27' south and the longitude is 148° 27' east.

If the passage through Bass's Strait is an object of desire, it is much better to keep to the northward after passing King's Island as far as latitude 39° 30' south; you then pass to the northward of the Sisters which are two small islands lying off the northerly end of Flinders Island. There is a chain of islands, rocks and shoals, the whole way along from the Sisters to Cape Barren Island, so that at any time, night or day no vessel would be safe to go amongst them.

Alec listened. Silence. A brooding, bitter lack of noise. Perhaps they could get back to work soon. Get some ducks and eels. Get ready for the return of the rest of the mob. He lowered his head to the transcription of Delano's journal.

All the islands of any magnitude in all these straits afford plenty of many kinds of game, such as kangaroo, badger, porcupine, and many species of waterfowls such as black swans, geese, several kinds of ducks, teals and a variety of beautiful birds in the woods and bushes. They provide a substantial larder for any ship that lands there.

Alec thought of the stories Uncle George told of his great Aunty Woonaji who he said lived on Cape Barren Island with old Mr West, one of Captain Mathews' men. Some said they'd died many years ago but Chub said no, he'd seen their fires, seen their fish traps, him and Stock picked up their fish every now and then and left flour and tea, few bottles, stuff like that. Stock said there were other people there too, warrigal Bunurong mob. Seen their canoes. Seen 'em corroboree. Stock was a bit like that Uncle Bung Eye, hard to know what he knew, what he saw, whose spirits he was in touch with. Dark horse that Stock. Kept his cards close to his chest. Them old sailors.

In my travels through the straits, I have on several occasions, fallen into the track of M. de la Perouse, and have had great

113

opportunity of knowing his merits, I think it is due to place him as one of the first navigators that the world has produced. He has explored more of the coast and islands from Kamshatka to the westward and southward as far as the island of Formosa, than perhaps all other navigators put together. In these straits he has been no less busy or exact.

I saw the ship, Ocean, *one of Collins' original fleet, but the Captain, Mathews, seemed less than open about his knowledge of the straits. It is my guess he is engaged in the sealing or other more nefarious occupations if the look of his piratical crew is any indication.*

On several occasions we saw natives going along the shore on the borders of the wood. They had three or four small, rudely constructed and ugly shaped canoes with them, with two outriggers each. The features of the people were far from disagreeable. Their skin was black and the hair as woolly as that on any native of Guinea. Several allowed themselves to be brought on board.

They had pretty good eyes, and their teeth were tolerably even, but very dirty. They looked on all our goods with complete indifference. The ship impressed them more for its being hollow than for any other feature of its design. The beads, coins and mirrors we tried to bestow upon them were thrown overboard with no civility whatsoever. I believe they are of incredibly low intelligence and will prove unreceptive to any of the refinements of civilisation.

Alec stared at the page. What did they expect us to find impressive? Their smelly arses. Their childish height? Their clothes? Tears of anger sprang from his eyes, tears of sorrow that so soon should his ancestors have been dismissed as beasts. As if the British ships were the first they'd seen. As if they didn't have better jewellery than the painted beads the Englishman offered.

But they got their way eventually. Look at Gavin and his bottles. They used their drugs to separate them from their spirit rather than bring them into unity with the spirit world. How dare they think themselves superior? How dare they convince our brothers of their worthlessness?

Gavin wrenched the door open and daylight sprang rudely into the room.

'What the fuck are you doin'?'

'Reading about the Straits.'

'Readin'. What business have you got with reading'?' Alec didn't reply. Anything he said could only be provocative. 'Eh? What are you readin' for, tryin' to become a gubba, eh? Crawl on ya guts to the white fella.'

'I'm gunna get a boat, Gav, like Chubber an' Stock, I'm gunna fish around the islands, sell 'em at Dalrymple. There's good money in it these days.'

'Money. Ya'll be a bloody gubba yaself 'fore long.'

'Least I'm not suckin' on their bottles, like a baby at the tit.'

'That so. Better'n me are ya? You the favourite son, are ya? Little fuckin' Christian.'

'Don't call me Christian. Never use that name against me.'

'Little Jesus, meek an' . . .'

Mildness was forgotten. Alec knew he was an idiot and he knew that to call someone a Christian was not the most cutting remark anyone could make to a sailor, but to a black sailor, and a black sailor from these particular islands it was the worst thing you could say and Gavin knew it and was sober enough now to reach for the fire poker as he said it.

Alec was up on his feet and throwing good punches at his brother's head, knowing that it was a stupid, stupid thing to do, that they'd allowed the white fellas to come between them and it couldn't end except with sorrow and bitterness.

And that was already on the way in the arc of Gavin's arm bringing the rod of steel, a remnant from some wreck or other, hard down on Alec's head. Except Alec reared away from the descending steel and would have escaped completely had not the tip clipped his eye and plucked it from the socket like an oystercatcher snatches the oyster.

Alec spun away and clamped a hand to his eye feeling the soft globe pressing against his palm. Gavin stepped outside the door and was gone. Alec leant against the fire mantle and considered what to do and his good eye fell on the journal he had been copying. What chance of a one eyed sailor being a skipper now? A one-eyed black sailor?

But Alec wasn't about to give up yet and looked about the hut for a bottle of spirit but Gavin would have made sure there wasn't any to be found either here or in any of the other huts. So for two days he camped by a small cove in the shelter of a bough screen and bathed his eye in salt water. He could get it back in the socket but he couldn't prevent the flies from discovering its corruption. He could switched them away and continued the routine of bathing even though he knew it was hopeless. The globe had been punctured, leaking fluid and puckering, empty. At last the smell told him his eye was dead so he took his knife, burnt it above the flame of his fire and severed the umbilical of his eye.

He bathed the socket and almost immediately he could feel the recovery. A hole in his head but at least it was beginning to seal itself. He cut the tongue out of his boot and made himself a patch, more like a pirate sailor than ever.

He drew his father's possum skin about him and lay by the fire, wreaths of smoke engulfing his face when the light winds quartered from the east, the smell of drift wood and eucalypt easing him, calming the nerves of his blind eye and the gentle sea rode its pony waves onto the coarse sand and pebbles of the beach, rolling them against each other with soft knocks and tocs, soughing through the coarse sand with each indrawn breath.

Breath, breath, breath said the sea; sigh, breath, sigh. The Bunurong-Palewa warrior slept with the sigh, sweep, breath and toc of the shore waves in his ears.

Breath, breath, breath said the sea to his dream, breath, sigh, breath, you will live our warrior, breath, breath, breath, we will cure you with our breath, breath, breath, we will never engulf you, we will always lift you up, you are our sailor seal, your seed will be sea beads, your babies will be anointed here, in this bay, we will send ponies to rock and buoy them, breath, breath, breath, our warrior, breath, breath, breath.

And the sea told Alec a big story. Bigger than the degrees and minutes, the leagues and fathoms of Amaso Delano, it told him of the giant patience of the sea and how it could engulf land almost absent-mindedly and then, in the way of slow giants, as if remembering itself, deliver up the land once again, surprising the corals and tube worms with air, so that the sea floor dried and blew up into great dunes, rippled like the roof of the giant's own gaping and snoring mouth. Dwell there and listen to him sleep, breath, breath, breath.

Alec dreamt of the soughing of the giant lungs and was nudged in his sleep. 'Gwennie,' he murmured. 'Urrrh,' she answered. Jesus, her breath stank. Alec opened his eye and peered into the great eye looking into his. 'Kurrman,' he said, 'Urrh,' she replied and his good eye closed as the smoke curled about him, sliding into the great and easeful sea sleep of the beach. The seal gazed at him, Christ he was ugly, a fur seal with some-one else's fur.

Four
DALRYMPLE

'Mrs Mathews?'

'Who are you?'

'Alec Hummock. From Flinders Island.'

'Hummock?'

'Yes.'

'Uncle George's son?'

'Yes.'

'Aunty Ida?'

'Yes.'

'How did you get here?'

'On the trader, *John Franklin*.'

'What do you want?'

'I want to study for the Masters' Certificate.'

'Mrs Kennedy says you've only got one eye.'

'Yes.'

'How can you be a captain?'

'I came to ask you, Mrs Mathews.'

'Well I can't. I'm dying, can't you see. I'm twice as blind as you. Leave me alone.' Alec didn't know what to do. The easiest thing was to stand still and look about the room of the white lady. 'Well, I said to leave me. I can't help you. There are others taking over the school now. Go and see them.'

'They said no.'

'Of course they did, we can't have blind captains.'

'I'm not blind.'

'One-eyed then. A port sided sailor. Have you been on ships before?'

'I was born by the sea, Mrs Mathews, my cousins are the Kennedys.'

'Chub?'

'Yes.'

'He's a good sailor, a good man.'

'So am I.'

'What's your name?'

'Alec.'

'Alec, I'm sorry, I need to be left alone. I'm at the very end of my life and I have only one wish and that wish seems to be withheld, so . . . so I'm tired now and just want to be left alone.'

'You want to see Johnny Mullagh, Mrs Kennedy told me. Chubber and Stock took young Caleb across to the mainland to try and bring him back.'

'Have you heard anything?' If she'd been well enough she would have raised herself on an elbow and peered at him through the fog of her remaining sight.

'No, no one's heard nothing.'

'No, I thought not.'

'Why don't you go to him?'

'I can't. Look at me.'

'You're dying, anyone can see that, but you may as well die looking.'

'Ridiculous.'

'I could take you.'

'No captain, no boat.'

'You've got a boat. I seen her pulled up on the beach.'

'*Dalrymple*? She's only a couta boat. She's old.'

'We cross the strait in them all the time. That's

119

all we got mostly.'

Eugenie lay still, listening to the shallow gulps of her puny lungs. Breath, ffff, breath.

'Don't need a captain's ticket for a couta boat.'

'I'd die out there.'

'Might. Might die here.'

At dawn on the flat Tamar estuary, the *Dalrymple* looked convincing enough, fore and aft sails plumped by the light breeze, the bow wave curving away like black glass with threads of reflected rose.

Alec stood at the tiller, deliberately looking to the horizon, captain-like, so that his gaze was averted from the stick woman bundled in a mound of scarves and rugs.

'Johnny used to take me on the estuary like this. Showed me the waterfall at Beauty Point. Are we past that now?' Alec didn't answer. 'Anyway it's gone now, it's a water race for the mill. Won't they get a surprise when they find me gone?' Not much of a surprise. Glancing over his shoulder Alec could see Mrs Kennedy still standing on the wharf. She'd provisioned the boat. Sandwiches, fruit, tea, smoked cuts of lamb, pickled eggs, a mound of rugs. And opium. Shown Alec how to put it on the old woman's tongue. The source of the sudden eloquence and dreaming wit.

'Johnny was a blackfella too you know.' Surprise, surprise. 'But of course, he's your cousin or something I suppose.' She could just touch her face with her fingers and drew a strand of brittle hair behind her ear. 'Do you realise that nobody has ever seen me naked?' They're not about to now, neither. 'Even my husband, Captain Mathews. Surprising isn't it?' Not according to Aunty Ida. 'But Johnny took me out here, taught me how to swim. Naked as the day I was born. I can still feel the water on me. I can hear it on the planks. Lovely isn't it.' Breath, breath, breath. 'I missed a great deal in my life, but I miss my father most. Do you miss yours?' Fellas like my father don't go missing, they just lose their bodies. 'Caleb was a good man, you know, that business with Belle, well those things can happen, perhaps I should have gone back to Sea Elephant. What do you think?' I think we're about to see how good this boat is. Or how good dead ladies swim.

They were coming outside the sheltering arm of the shoals off Low Head. 'And I miss Johnny. He taught me not to fear the water. Taught me to love the land, not just live on it. Defy it. You, you probably think this is nonsense, madness, but that was a big lesson for me. It came too late for me, but in time others will learn to love this place. Unless they defy it. Try to bend it to their will. But your people, what do your people think?' My people think that if this north-easter holds we might make Franklin Sound without getting too wet. 'The school you see, once I'd started the school I had people depending on me, your people too you know, and I couldn't leave. But I didn't want to either. There's something about the honeysuckle in places like this. Something about the perfume, the way it mixes with the sea. Have you noticed that?' Alec remembered the breath of the seal, urrh. 'I didn't want to leave, the evenings were like a drug to me . . . like I was meant to be here . . . and now I'm meant to find Johnny Mullagh one more time. Where are we?' On the sea, we're on the sea and our bow is handling the shore swells as good as you could hope. 'Where are we?'

'We're off Low Head, missus, we're clear of the shoals, heading north-east. Should be in the Sound before dark.'

'Is there a toilet?' Is there a toilet? It's a tin pan and over the side, madam.

'At Flinders there is, but otherwise there's just this.' And Alec held up the tin pan. She caught the dull glint of the cold metal. Mmmm. 'I can help you a bit, but then, it's up to you. I'm sorry, missus, but it'll be like that most of the time. We mightn't even land at Flinders. It'd be hard to get you on and off the boat . . . until you're a bit stronger.'

'I'll stink.' Alec thought of the seal, urrh.

'No one'll notice out here, missus.' Unless the wind changes.

Dalrymple, well she was named after the old port, made out of great planks of Huon pine, beech struts, lovely blackwood fore and aft decks. Bit splintery now, the sails brown like dry kelp, but she was dry, a good clean hand had fashioned this bow. Plenty weren't, but the *Dalrymple* was shaped so the bow plunged into each wave deflecting the spray as a girl sweeps hair from her face and now a bit like an old lady stroking away her dying hair with her claw. The action hadn't been lost on Alec's averted gaze. He'd noticed the girl bones slender within the hook of her shrivelling hand, the winsomeness of the face as the hair was drawn from it. Someone should have loved that face, thought Alec, who was as soft, as searching . . . as his father. When he thought of the face of Mrs Mathews, he didn't think winsome, in fact he didn't have a word for it, but he thought someone should have loved that face, someone should have loved that woman enough so that in her last days she wasn't undertaking a dubious crossing of one of the worst stretches of water in the world.

Alec fed *Dalrymple* through the banks and shoals of the Sound like a seamstress feeling for the gap in the threads. They were able to shelter off Kent Bay where Alec could see a single light in Aunty Ida's hut far across the Sound and wondered what Gavin was doing. A thought slipped through his mind, like the dart of a swallow, that he could have brought back a bottle for his brother, but then he didn't have a shilling to his name, and besides, the bottles didn't bring Gavin comfort, just raised the devils of his disappointment and bitterness. But he shouldn't have called me a gubba. Me own brother should never have called me that. All of us is a bit white now, all got a bit of strait's sealer like Aunty Ida says, but it doesn't make us white. He should never have said that.

The tin pan came into use and Alec helped as well and discreetly as he could but, it was true, the old lady smelt like a rookery of dead penguins.

'I'm sorry. I stink.' Eugenie said.

'It's alright, Mrs Mathews, we all stink.'

'Not like this. Not like me. What's your name?'

'Alec.'

'You're mad, Alec. Shipping a corpse across the Strait.'

'You'll be right, Mrs Mathews.'

'No I won't, Alec. No I won't at all. I wish I hadn't come. I feel so bad. Mrs Kennedy had some . . .'

'She gave it to me, missus. Here, look, I can put it on your tongue.'

'Like Canton. There are rooms over there where people grow up, live and die with the seed.'

'You'll be right, missus.'

'No, I won't.'

The couta boat rose and fell with the swell, pointing at the wind, riding on the anchors, a dark slip on the sea, two bundles fore and aft, heaped and rugged, one of them murmuring a story that sent the other one to sleep.

'Canton. Kowloon, oh, you should have smelt those harbours, Eric. The perfume, the spice, the stink. We could sail there now couldn't we, sail off in the *Dalrymple* like the owl and the pussycat in their beautiful pea green boat.' *Dalrymple*'s as grey as a mollyhawk and we'll be lucky if we see another piece of land after this. I'll be swimmin' but I don't know about you.

'The Owl and the Pussycat went to sea in a beautiful pea green boat. Which of us is the owl and which the pussycat, Eric?' I'll be the seal if it's alright with you, madam, and it's Alec. 'Hey, which of us is the owl? It's a shame about Caleb you know. He was a good man. As men get. But . . . well, I've had trouble with men, Eric, trouble with the concept of men.' Alec saw the tiny movement of her claw describing an arc against the chaos of the great belt of southern stars. 'After Ireland, Eric, after that I wasn't much taken with men and what they did. Are you married, Eric?'

'Alec, missus, me name is Alec. I'm gunna be, I'm gunna marry Gwennie, I hope.'

'You hope?'

'Aunty Ida said I had to see you and become a captain before I could get married.'

'You'll never be a captain, Eric, not with one eye. Neither of us will ever be captains now, Eric, one eye between us. And what would you have done with your Masters' Certificate?'

'Fished, missus. Fished the islands. Done a bit of freight. Would have been handy for the island, see.'

'Yes, yes, you need something like that, so far away. What about Chub and Stock?'

'They go off down the west coast for months at a time. Go out of Stanley. If I'd got mine we'd always have a boat hereabouts.'

'Well, Eric, what about the *Dalrymple*. She'd do the job and you wouldn't need a skipper's certificate . . . as long as you could stand sailing a boat where an old lady had died.'

'You'll be right, missus.'

'No I won't, Eric, and you may call me Eugenie at the end of my life.'

'And mine's Alec, not Eric, Mrs Mathews.'

'Alright Alec, but Eugenie, please call me Eugenie. I want to hear it said these last few days.'

'Mum would kill me, missus. No respect.'

'Respect . . . Alec, respect, respect is helping an old lady clean herself. I think you're the pussycat, Alec, I think you are. The owl and the pussycat went to sea in Alec's brand new boat.'

'They'll take it off me, Mrs Mathews.'

'I'll write it, Alec. Look, see my hand, I can still wave my hand about.'

He could barely see the claw etching a skittery wave against the squid-ink sky.

'In the morning we'll write it. And to my friend, Alec Hummock, the pussy cat, the beautiful sea green *Dalrymple*.' He could see the fingers fluttering about. Thank Christ for the poppy.

Most of the night she murmured and fluttered, the Milky Way, a blur like a cataract on her failing eyes. Mullet slapped the water, bream shoaled, sharks snooped, Alec slept.

My children, Yolla's chickens on the mutton bird rookery, woke him with their shrieks and squalls and the first thing he saw was the claw clutching the gunwale and to his shame his first thought was, I hope that hand is still alive because I want it to write. He sat up to see if there was life.

'Is that you awake, Alec?'

'Yes, Mrs Mathews.'

'I have need of your pannikin, Alec, but more particularly the white powder if you don't mind.'

When she opened her mouth the gums and teeth seemed separated from her jaw, she was so gaunt and drawn, the flesh of her face caved in against the pain, the eyes huge, blind but staring from their sockets.

'Here you are, Mrs Mathews. I've put the powder in your mouth.' The tongue seemed to have shrunk and it rolled the powder like a cockatoo with banksia seeds. There was a long silence. Alec busied himself preparing *Dalrymple* to set sail as soon as the sun was high enough to light their way. His hand was on the anchor when he heard her voice like the mewing of a wet kitten.

'Alec.'

'Yes, missus?'

'The paper, remember. And a pen. In my little bag. And I'll need that pan. I've soiled myself, I believe.' But she hadn't, she'd bled. Great gouts of it like afterbirth. Alec did his best. Jaw and thorax taut as a hawser against the stench. He bathed her with a cloth dipped in the sea. She watched his eyes.

'You're a brave man, Alec.'

'It's alright, missus.'

'No it's not. It's not at all, but you are a gentleman. Now get me that pen and paper. And I think you're right, you should be very careful with this paper, put it in a bank, somewhere . . . they may not believe.' She straightened as best she could so that her wavering hand could get the best angle because if this paper was worth anything it had to look like it was written by a school teacher – not a rogue fisherman, a black fisherman. History hadn't been kind to their witness.

The pen scratched as the birds wheeled and dipped against the rising sea. I, Mrs Eugenie Mathews, deed this boat, the *Dalrymple*, to my friend, Alec Hummock of Flinders Island for his use and ownership. April 3, 1854.

'There, that should do. Now keep it safe, Alec, and let's on with the voyage . . . but perhaps some more powder, Alec, the writing has tired me.'

She said very little as they wound their way out of the Sound. At one stage Alec looked back and saw a figure at the jetty looking after them. Alec didn't raise his arm but steered the *Dalrymple* beyond the island shoals before turning the bow to the north.

Eugenie murmured from time to time in her opiate dream.

'Butterflies, Eric, butterflies.'

'Yolla, Mrs Mathews, mutton birds.'

'Oh, Yolla. Yolla, Yolla lives in squalor.' Opium is for poets, but the birds, moonbirds some call us, sheared the wind off the face of the waves dipping and soaring, sometimes slipping the wind past Eugenie's face.

'Yolla butterflies, Eric.'

But that Alec, he had his face set into the north-east trying to get the angle right so that her smell would be taken to port. He didn't feel comfortable around this decay.

All day the *Dalrymple* plunged against the swell

and all day my children scoured the waves plucking the whitebait and squid from the crests, preparing themselves for their own northern journey. They might be flying to Siberia but Eugenie Mathews' voyage was no less epic.

Alec sensed there was no purpose in contemplating anything but the set of sail and trim of bow. How long the old lady would last was anyone's guess. Sometimes these old Irish birds clutched on to life like the transparent chrysalis of cicadas, frail, weightless and bug-eyed.

He caught snatches of Irish reel, poetry, girlish gibberish, and sometimes a sober question.

'Did your people know the world was round, Alec?' Well if you can sail out of sight of land and back again it has to be round, doesn't it?

'Even from Cape Barren, you can see the curve, missus. We knew it had to be round, or a bit round. Uncle George said stuff like that.'

'Thought you said he was your father.'

'Uncle, too. Blackfella way.'

But most of the time she wasn't lucid at all. The claw would clutch the gunwale and he'd move forward and administer the powder.

It was late in the day when they came in sight of Deal Island and he saw her face incline toward the west as they made to pass the island.

'I can hear surf, Eric.'

'It's the island, Mrs Mathews, Deal Island, where the new lighthouse is.'

'Caleb's island?'

'That's right. Galub's lighthouse. Chub and Stock call in and keep him supplied with all he needs. Keeps to himself pretty much. He's blind.'

'We're all blind. One eye between the three of us. Your one eye and the sun, all we have to see by.'

'Meera.'

'What's that you said?'

'Meera. The sun. The eye. Mean the same thing.'

'The eye and the sun.'

Chub and Stock had told Alec that they had never seen Captain Mathews outside. They landed beside the crude landing, hooked the stores onto a windlass and blew the ship's horn. Eventually the goods would be hauled up the cliff face and a flag would flutter from the guys of the light tower. That was all. Once or twice in fine weather, when Chub was happy to leave *Yolla* in Stock's hands at the landing for an hour, he had ascended with the stores in the cargo net.

He didn't have the words to describe the Deal Island Light. It didn't need height because it was perched on a naked bulb of granite, easily seen from all directions. It was a squat stone tower with an even more squat store house at its foot. The house scared Chub. There was a fire, warm enough, sufficient food if you like tea, tobacco, rice and ships' biscuits, there was a chair with a cushion made of flour bags stuffed in a flour bag. On the table was a whale oil lantern, a teapot, a cup and a large ledger.

'A cup of tea?' Captain Mathews asked on the first occasion. And that was about it. Some detailed discussion of weather, tides, shipping and boats, not an ounce of curiosity about the state of the world. Not an ounce. He watched, as a blind man watches, slightly askew, while Chub drank his tea. There was only one cup.

`Your ship?' he asked on that first occasion.

'*Yolla*, Captain Mathews.'

'Good, I'll write it in the log.' But didn't move a finger. He knew some of the ships by their whistle, and some by the goods they clipped onto his cargo net, so his log made a kind of intermittent sense, but eventually the authorities would discover he was blind and kick him off. But they wouldn't find out from a sailor. Certainly not Chubber Kennedy.

As *Dalrymple* sailed past, Captain Mathews heard the crack of sail but couldn't recognise her. 'Unknown vessel. April 3, 1854. 1600. Northerly passage.' He could hear the sail whip and the lanyards creaking in that direction.

'He was a good man. Don't let anyone say otherwise, Eric.' Eugenie opined from her opium couch.

'He's alone.' Alec murmured but not so soft for the ears of a dying woman.

'We're all alone, Eric, all of us. Look at me, look at him, look at you.'

'I'm not alone.'

'Yes, you have your people. That is true, but Eric, what are you doing sailing a white woman's boat.'

'Alec.'

'What?'

'My name, it's Alec.'

'But what is your real name, eh? What are you and your people sailing into, Alec? It's not just me and the Captain who are sailing blind.'

She said very little for the rest of the evening, lulled by the drug and weakness.

There was no light on the jetty at Sea Elephant but Alec was able to guide himself from the oil lamp gleaming in the old Captain's shack where Aunty Ida now shaped the map of her family's destiny over the passing of teapots, roast duck, fish, mutton birds and geese. The preparation of food could not pass without a memory being stripped out with the gut of fish or fowl.

But it was late. Aunty Ida was on her last pot of tea for the night. Or second last anyway. Only Veronica was at the jetty watching the horizon for sails and this late at night for the phosphorescence gleaming from a bow wave.

She saw the silhouette of a head as the boat approached. Unmistakable.

'Alec, what you doin' here?'

'I got a boat.'

'Whose boat?'

'Mine. Watch out, I'm comin' in on the leeside. Grab the bow rope.'

'What's that in the bow, Alec?'

'It's Mrs Mathews.'

'Jesus.'

'She's crook.'

'Well, what's she doin' out here? And what's wrong with your eye?'

'Get Mum, I don't know what to do.' Veronica ran to get the old lady while Alec made the boat fast and then sat back against the bollard waiting for his mother to devise a plan.

'What's this you got, Alec?' He could hear her even before she'd got down to the jetty. 'What's this all about? And where's your eye?'

'I'll tell you later, Mum, it's alright I can still see. Good enough to sail.'

'And who's that then?

'It's Mrs Mathews, she give me her boat.'

'Well that's as it may be, but what's she doin' in it?'

'She's lookin' for Johnny Mullagh.'

'She should be home. What you doin' to that old lady, Alec?'

'I told you, she's lookin' for Johnny.'

'It's the owl and the pussycat, Aunty Ida, the owl and the pussycat. Eric has kindly brought me on a voyage.'

'She's mad as a cut snake,' Aunty Ida muttered to Veronica. 'He should never've brung you out to sea, Mrs Mathews,' she said louder, leaning down to peer at the bundle in the bow of the *Dalrymple*. And caught a whiff of her.

'Strewth,' she whistled through her teeth.

'I'm dying, Aunty Ida, but Eric's been very kind, very much the gentleman. And I'm on my last voyage, like Cleopatra on her barge.'

'Barge or no barge, we'll have to get you up to the house.' Aunty Ida scrambled down into the boat and began to unlayer the rugs and blankets while Veronica, on the jetty held the lamp above them. They all heard Aunty Ida's indrawn breath. 'Well perhaps you might be more comfortable in the boat for the time being, Mrs Mathews, perhaps you might.'

'She might need some of her medicine, Mum,' said Alec holding it out to his mother. Aunty Ida sniffed it and glanced up at the dark silhouette of her son's face. Noting the even darker shadow of his socket.

'You had any of this?'

'No, Mum.'

'Sure?'

'Haven't touched none of it.'

'Good. Here, Mrs Mathews, better have a bit of medicine before we make you comfy for the night.' Aunty Ida administered a portion of the drug and then climbed the ladder back to the jetty and gestured for Alec to follow. 'How long's she been like that?'

'Dunno. Ever since we left, I suppose.'

'And what about your eye?'

'Just an accident.'

'And you can see?'

'Yes.'

'What kind of accident?'

'Bit of wire.'

'Wire, eh. Tell me later. What about her? How much of that powder's she had?'

'Plenty.'

'And the blood?'

'Plenty.'

'For how long?'

'Since this morning.'

'And you reckon she wants to get to the mainland?'

'Yes.'

'You sure?'

'Yes, she's lookin' for Johnny.'

'Alright, but what about the boat?'

'She wrote a paper for it.'

'Did you ask her?'

'No, Mum, she wanted me to have it. She knows she's dying. The boat hasn't been used much for years. She's nearly a wreck.'

'Not too much of a wreck to sail the Strait.'

'Bit of caulking and paint, she'll be good-o.'

'Alright Alec, Vronica, you listenin'. You give me that paper and we'll get Errol to copy it out for us, you know what he's like with is drawin', but you've gotta get to Port Albert as quick as you can and speak to that mob there. There's . . .'

'The owl and the pussycat went to sea in their beautiful pea green boat, with lots of honey and . . .'

'Thank Christ for that powder. I've seen sealers who've lost a leg or arm on the windlass singing out like that after a dose of the poppy.

'Now there's the Bunurong mob at Port Albert, work on the boats there. You've gotta get them to send a message to my Aunty Kneebone up on the river to track down Johnny and young Caleb . . . if they're still alive. But somehow you've got to stop gubbas seein' you with a white lady. There's a little creek on that Kadak Island, you know that one? Snake, Uncle George's mob fish there. Hide the boat up in that creek until you get word from Aunty Kneebone. But if Mrs Mathews dies first, you better get her back here quick smart and then we'll think what to do. An' if she dies you smoke her, alright.'

'Yes, Mum.'

'No, yes Mum, you fill this boat with green leaves an' you smoke her, smoke this boat good an' proper or she'll be the death of you. This is important, Alec, I don't want my son drownin' all for the sake of a white woman's spirit. Now, come here and hug your mother, hug ya sister too. Vronica, you go an' get him plenty to eat. Get those ducks outa the coals and wrap 'em up fa Alec. Give him a bottle of the Captain's fancy plonk, too. Not too bad that stuff, when ya get used to it. Alright, Alec. If she lives two days it'll be a miracle. Get the boat ready. What's she called?'

'*Dalrymple*.'

'Hmm. Alright, get her ready. You haven't got time to sleep here tonight. Don't drink that bottle until you meet up with them Bunurong. Them Briggses. They'll help you. But that passage through them sandbars is mean so keep your eyes open. Sorry. Tell me about the eye later. And Alec?'

'Yes, Mum.'

'Come back.'

'I'll be right. I've been havin' a doze on the way across. She sails like a dream, this one.'

'Well no dozin' when you get near that passage into the port, that's all.'

'Lots of honey and a little bit of . . .'

'Jesus. Here's Vronica, anyway. Take the stuff and get goin'.'

'. . . tied up in a one pound note.'

'Mad as a cut snake. If she's alive by dawn it'll be a miracle, Vronica.'

'Alec will look after her.'

'It'll be her Lord will be doin' the lookin' after, I hope. And who will look after Alec?'

Me. They call us moonbird. Yolla bird. Come the moon and we're off. March, April or such. With the moon. And here she is. Yern. All them Yolla are scudding across the waves, picking the wind off the rise of the sea, like wide black warheads, like them mulga boomerang thrown by a good arm. And Yern gives us the light, silvering the sea, bringing up the yournit so my children can fill their belly on the waves one last time and here she is the death barge, the *Dalrymple*, the phosphorescence showering from the bow and that black man, a dark stick at the stern, and that mad voice coming from a bundle of rugs in the bow.

'Slowly, silently now the moon,
walks the night in her silver shoon,
this way and that she peers and sees
. . . silver mutton birds on silver seas.'
Silence.
'Silver mutton birds, Eric.'

'Yes, Mrs Mathews. Beautiful.'

'Yes, yes, beautiful, beautiful. Thank you, Eric. Thank you for the silver night.'

'It's not mine, missus, we're just in it.'

'Quite, quite so. What a beautiful ship she is, don't you think?'

'She sails like a dream, missus.'

'Yes, indeed, like a dream. Be true to her for me, Eric.'

Alec reminded himself to check the paper to make sure she'd written Alec and not Eric.

'I can see the Curtises, Mrs Mathews, we'll be into the shoals off the port before long.'

'Shoals.'

'Near Kadak Island.'

'Kadak?'

'Snake.'

'Oh yes, the snake. For ever and a day.'

The rose of dawn was clouded by my children crossing the path of the rising sun in their passage to the other side of the globe while three slim black shapes paddled from the main land in response to Alec's fire on Kadak Island. The occupants landed at the far end of the beach and listened to the strange voice.

'The owl and the pussycat went to sea
in their beautiful pea green boat
with plenty of honey and lots of money
wrapped up in a ten pound note.

Oh fabulous pussy, oh pussy my love . . .'

The black men looked down into the boat and then greeted Alec silently.

'She's come to find Johnny Mullagh. She grew him up. We sent young Caleb over to find him on the Murray.'

'Has Johnny come? Is he here?' the faint voice called.

'Aunty Ida said to send a message up to Aunty Kneebone.'

'She mirrouk, wanung, she mirrouk bye an' bye.'

'I know. I give her this medicine.'

'What happen she die?'

'Bury her. Smoke her, Aunty Ida said.'

'Yes, yes, the smoke. Is that you Johnny? I knew you'd come.'

'I'll give her some medicine and try and wait for them to get the message.'

'Is that you, Johnny?'

'Here, missus, here's the powder.'

'Oh, Johnny, I knew you'd come. Oh, Johnny at last, at last. You see, Eric has been very good to me. The *Dalrymple* is his now. Remember you taking me to Beauty Point in her? Say you remember, Johnny.'

There was a long silence. Karborer looked into the boat for a long time and then lifted his eyes slowly to his nephew, pouting his lips in the raving woman's direction.

'Yes, Mum,' Alec said as he took the cue from his uncle. 'Yes, Mum, I remember.'

'I knew you would, Johnny, I knew you would. Hold my hand, my darling.' The claw waved uncertainly from the rugs, like the hallucinatory weave of the mantis. Alec took the hand trying not to scramble the collection of bones. 'Oh, Johnny, I knew you'd come. I knew you would. One thing, Johnny, I ask one thing. Look after yourself, my son . . . and look after Eric . . . and the river, Johnny, look after it, love it like you taught me. Say you will, Johnny.'

'Yes, Mum.'

'Kiss me.'

Alec leant over her. The face was narrow like a fox skull, hair springing from it like a cheap doll. He kissed her.

'Thank you, Johnny.'

The blackfellows stared intently at the woman, wondering, never having seen a white person die.

If at a death you are not watching for something very particular you begin to move from foot to foot, uneasily, waiting to be released, waiting for your cue to leave, but if you are trained to watch for the emergence of the spirit then you have no impatience, the vigil has no time, no time at all.

Finally, Karborer saw it go and his fellows murmured and pointed by barely crooking their fingers and sighing on the exhalation of a breath.

'Mirrouk, mirrouk.'

The blur and whirr of wings hummed like a quiet bullroarer around them as my spirit children passed, intent on their own journey, and in their midst somewhere, the confused spirit of a white woman hovered and hesitated before being taken by the smoke of Alec's fire to drift faintly toward the mainland across the shoals and channels of an emerald and blue-black sea.

The men cut boughs from the low scrub of the island and held them over the fire, beating themselves about the body and limbs before placing them around the corpse and the hull of *Dalrymple* as she lay aslant on the beach of the island of the great snake.

Five yellow-tailed black cockatoos, wirran, flew above the trees in that slow creaking, gliding and dipping flight, riding the cushion of air above the green crowns of the forest calling, wirran, wirran.

Two dark skinned men glanced at them, recognising their voice, but not faltering in their passage south. They were coming. Johnny Mullagh and Caleb Mathews were on their way. You'd say they were late because sons should always hold their dying mother's hand. There's a neatness about it which some cultures crave, but it rarely happens like that. They were late for some things and just in time for others.

Karborer and his brothers collected paperbark and took it to the little estuary to which Alec had drawn the *Dalrymple*. The mast was taken out of the step and she was paddled up the channel overarched by the tea-tree and wattle.

Eugenie Mathews was well loved by the people of the Strait who knew her by her kindness to their people but that's not why they afforded her the honour of choosing the sacred paperbark for her shroud. It was simple expedience. The disease had so corrupted her body and the weather in April was still warm so that disintegration was well underway. The paperbark would bind her for long enough so that Alec could get her back to Sea Elephant. For one romantic minute Alec had considered Deal Island, a return to her husband, but images of hauling her up on the cargo sling in her unstable state were enough to quell the thought.

They laboured throughout the day to bind the old woman and tie green leaves to the gunwale but *Dalrymple* would not be able to sail until nightfall, too risky, the trail of smoke would attract the attention of any other ship on the sea and there was hardly a ship's master afloat who would believe that a black man owned a boat, especially if the previous owner was dead in the bow.

They cooked mussels and oysters on a small fire while they waited for the night to arrive but just on sunset five wirran flew above them, feinted at a passage out to sea, then turned in a great dipping arc and settled in a grove of banksias by the outlet of the small estuary, crying in their weird voice reserved for such things, eeer, eeer, eeer, eeer.

At last Alec poled the *Dalrymple* down the stream,

stepped the mast, lit the smoking torches, set the sail and glided in and out the sandbars towards the outer strait. Karborer and his brothers stood on the headland beneath the banksias where they were joined by two young black men who looked out towards the *Dalrymple* trailing a pall of smoke in the moonlight, slipping behind the silhouette of the outer reef. Eeer, eeer, eeer.

So, she was dead. Johnny watched the slim smoke trail of her death barge. The others returned to the preparations of their night camp but he continued to watch until all that could be seen was a dirty smudge against clouds lit by fading sunset.

He didn't know what to think or what to feel. So much had been taken from his people there was already too much to mourn, so that the grief for the surrogate mother he genuinely loved just felt like emptiness, just one more experience of theft. He should cry but knew it would be from frustration and anger rather than a son's grief. So he didn't. Just stood and watched the stain of smoke.

He could follow her, stand by the grave, but what then? He was sick of seeing his people caught in a cycle of mourning, grieving for this one dead by the gun, this one by the plague, this one by a broken heart. And every time they lost more, all the time they spent grieving the whitefellas spent stealing.

Did he have time to spend by another graveside? He had an idea and fully aware that part of the idea was white. But that's how he was, he could feel it, half'n'half, but at least he knew enough of the white world to protect his idea from attack, to plan, buy time to put the plan into action.

He stood watching the horizon, unaware now if smoke still drifted against the darkening sky. And what else was there to do? Learn a few Christian hymns, wear someone's clothes become too small because of the corpulence stolen from his land? Sit down, dream of the past, mourn the passing of those who could no longer endure the incredible pain of absence?

The old men knew he listened to things someone of his age should never hear, but he was just a half'n'half, that's what the old fellas thought, they couldn't initiate him in the law no matter how they bent the rules, it didn't matter what half'n'half heard. So he heard the stony sounds of their grief for country. Single words uttered from tight throats late at night while others slept. He'd heard them talk, the old ones, heard each one name a place on the trail of their song, nothing else, just the name: Moorooduc, Tooradin, Balnarring, Tyabb, Werribee, Corio, Jillong, Mordialloc, Almurta, Wonthaggi, Korumburra, Tara, Toora, Tynong, Yanakie, all them Bunurong names, and all of them lost, he'd heard them all breathed across the fire and followed by silence and the awful unspoken witness to what had been lost there, not just the lives of men and women gutted by gunshot, but the life that was lost, the way of life, the increasing impossibility of maintaining the law with so many elders gone, with young men and women crowded into mission houses and drunken slums, this clan and that clan all confused, no one to receive the new babies and cradle them in arms, to separate the hairs on their head, feeling the hair, deciding whether this baby is eagle or crow, finding its designated place, its destiny, its birthright.

Babies born and no one knowing where they were from, what was right for them, how to determine their role in the great cycle of life they had inherited.

You couldn't breathe the names of the dead, just the places where they'd been and that was enough, everyone understood the shorthand, and the enormous grief made the firelight quaver, it was palpable, flames choked on their pyre, engulfed by the awful surge of hearts that knew they had lost. Everything.

And Johnny knew he was one of those who had never been cradled by the right people, never had the hairs on his baby head examined by elders of the law, and their grief was his loss. Because they had given up, the chain was all but broken and they would take their secrets with them, unable to pass it on to these crude, pale young, who might be able to recite all the psalms, write them on paper, but didn't know where they had come from or why and what they were meant to do.

Johnny could see the old ones dying by the fire, their secrets like stones lodged in their throats, choking them, and it made him feel fury, literally become blind with anger whenever he thought of what was lost, and the greatest pain of all, and he knew the old people felt this, was the insult that these supposedly superior beings could not see the neatness of their way of doing things, the fairness of it, the overpowering respect given to life and spirit, that these Christians, these devout servants of a spiritual life, could not witness the hand of God at work, could not contemplate an eighth day when God woke up rested and got it right, discovered fairness and put it in a black skin.

But Johnny dismissed these thoughts of his anger, it was no good slumping into despondency, he intended to fight. He couldn't dwell on the conundrum of mutually incomprehensible civilisations, something had to be done before one of them was lost forever on the altar of the other's ignorance.

He would follow Eugenie's funeral barge because he'd never been allowed the grace of being at his real mother's funeral, but that was all, he could spare grief no more time than that for he intended to fight.

Fight like the devil.

Alec and Veronica did most of the work while Uncle George sat out by the reef singing a song none of them had ever heard. Aunty Ida recognised the words mirrouk and brinbeal but was unsure of the rest except to realise that Eugenie Mathews was being paid great respect. She was on her way. None of her own to see her there, of course, none to guffaw at an old white lady bundled in heathen paperbark, perhaps that was just as well.

Gwennie sat a little away from the hole being dug, too advanced in her pregnancy to be much use to anyone, feeling more like a jellyfish than a woman, and wondering, wondering of the time when a hole would be dug for her and if the people who dug it would be strangers. She stared at Alec, had been staring at him for some minutes, before he finally looked up. He paused, wiped sweat from the corners of his eyes, blinking at the saltiness and caught her gaze upon him, this young woman with a belly like a seal.

What did she want? Why was she staring? Veronica bumped him with her hip, just enough to topple him against the side of the pit. She glanced at Gwennie and in the briefest instant caught Alec's eye and in bending to scrape more rubble from the hole nudged him again. He climbed out and looked out to the reef where Uncle George was still singing and then returned his gaze to Gwennie, who had never let her eyes shift from him.

'It's finished, just about,' he said to her. 'You hungry, want a drink?' He sat beside her and she moved her weight to fill the space between his hip and shoulder, as a cow will lean against the dairyman. Let him take the weight, it's all his fault.

'No.'

'Feelin' crook?'

'No.'

'What then? What are ya lookin' at me for? 'Veronica bent to a finicky straightening of the grave walls, but missed nothing, wondering herself what was to be said at such a moment.

'Nuthin'.'

'Nuthin'?'

'Just nuthin'. Just wanted you to sit with me. Let me lean against you. We're havin' a baby.'

'That's news.'

'It'll grow up . . . and I'm wondering how it'll be, Alec, you an' me ya know. What'll become of our baby, and us.'

Alec said nothing. Could think of nothing to say but stare across the reef to the ocean. Thought for a long time, trying to make some sense of it, let the woman weight bear in softly against his ribs.

'Bopup'll grow up on his land, Gwennie, with his people, grow up on the land that knows him.'

'And will he always have a father?'

'I told you that Gwennie,' he glanced across at Veronica's back and lowered his voice, 'I told ya I loved ya and that's that. That's all there is to it. I love ya.'

He loves her, thought Veronica. Isn't that what we want, not to die alone with people diggin' a hole for us who might be respectful enough, but in their blood they are strangers. And in her groin her own blood welled up in a great tide and she fell to her knees on the clay and clasped herself to herself in the absence of her man, who if he'd been there would have been dragged down on to her, grave or no grave, clay or no clay, and she would have pulled him into her, hauled on his arse, demanded that he prove it, prove he was her man.

Gwennie and Alec listened to the strange voice of Uncle George singing something to the sea and they wondered why Veronica was gurgling in the bottom of the pit with clay all over her face.

Respect. Aunty Ida wasn't sure if the respect was being paid to the old headmistress or to her two almost sons, Caleb and Johnny.

Alec leant an elbow on the table propping his jaw on the heel of his hand with the thumb and first two fingers covering the socket where his right eye used to be, a habit she'd noted as soon as he arrived with the corpse.

They sat together, mother and son, drinking the

black tea, strong and aromatic as pitch. Alec fiddled with a spoon in his cup, but Aunty Ida looked out through the four-paned window to the bay, listening to the breath of the sea, mumbling its gums over beach and reef like an old man on a rusk. Breath, breath, breath. Alec heard it too and for the first time in days thought of Flinders and his brother. His index finger smoothed the skin of his eye socket. He wanted to go home, get all his people back together on their land, even if Gavin was still there.

Aunty Ida saw the uncertain shape appear on the horizon and watched its steady approach. Even when it was still well outside the reef she knew that the paddlers had ochred their hair white and as the canoe slipped inside the bay she could see the bars and hoops on face and chest. Respect.

Over the rim of her cup she shifted her gaze to where Uncle George was sitting on the beach waiting. She in her turn watched and waited to see if there was an inflexion of lips or chin, but there was nothing. The black men did not speak. Karborer, Johnny Mullagh and Caleb the younger simply stepped over the outriggers of their canoe and followed Uncle George's path along the beach and onto the headland which had been selected for the white woman's grave.

'They're here,' Aunty Ida said.

'I heard,' Alec replied but didn't look up.

'What those blackfellas do now, you reckon?'

'Business.'

'Blackfella business?'

Alec said nothing.

'Better get goin' then, I suppose,' the old lady said but made no move. 'Better put that old lady in the ground.'

'We goin' home after this?' Alec looked at his mother, took his fingers from his socket and angled his head to turn the good eye her way. 'We go back home after this, Mum?'

'Haven't heard from Chub yet, about them mission mob.'

'I'm gunna write a letter to the guvna, tell him to leave us alone, give us a bit of land.'

'What land?'

'Barren, Flinders.'

'Hmmph.'

'There's laws. Like the paper for Dalyrmple. We get it on paper, it's law.'

'Give us our own land back?'

'Mum, we got nothin' otherwise. I'm gunna write a letter.'

'You speak to that old man of mine first.'

'He's Bunurong.'

'Respect, Alec, you gotta show that ol' fella respect.'

'I will. I'll speak to him. But I'm gunna write, get Chub to help me.'

'And they'll write back and say, certainly you blackfellas, certainly my dear chaps, here, here's a whole island, it's got the best harbour and the best seals but it's yours, from the bottom of our hearts.'

'Or we could run away to sea every time we hear a policeman or missionary is on the way. Run away every time we see a sail.'

'I don't trust them.'

'They trust paper. I'm gunna get some paper. Get Chub and Mrs Kennedy to help . . . maybe Captain Mathews.'

'Blind owls can't write.'

'He can write. Chub's seen it.'

'But what's he writin' up there in his stone lighthouse, what's he writin' that'll help us, Alec? He's a white man. He's a sealer, Alec, he's the one who started all this.'

'Not just him.'

'But he was there, he knew what was happenin', he shot our people remember.'

'But time's have changed . . .'

'Time, Alec, time never changes. Things get lost, things get found, but time just passes, Alec, and then you're dead. Time has the last word.'

'So we just let 'em chase us from one island to another.' Silence. Breath, breath, breath. 'I'm gunna write a letter. Plenty of letters.'

'You tell 'em how much you want Flinders, Alec, what a good place it is, and that's when they'll want it for themselves.'

'So, what, give up?'

'I dunno, son, I dunno. I don't have no faith in those people.'

'I'm gunna learn to write proper letters. Ask Chub to sell our fish and help me to write them letters.'

After the burying they stretched the grass mats on the sand while Veronica built the fire. Gwennie took the kids out to the rocks to collect abalone and crayfish.

Aunty Ida settled herself in a possum rug next to Uncle George.

'Alec's gunna write some letters. Try and get 'em to let us have the island.'

'Which island?' Veronica asked.

'Barren. So they can't push us off.'

'Letters,' Johnny Mullagh said.

'Amerjiyt,' said Uncle George.

'Well,' Aunty Ida said, 'you got any better ideas?'

'We back in that Barmah country, right back in the forest. We don' need no letters.' Johnny Mullagh said, a proud tone in his voice.

'Who's we?' Aunty Ida said watching her daughter settle the billy into the coals of the glowing fire.

'Yorta people. Big mob in that Barmah. No amerjiyt come in that country.'

'Yet.'

'We don't need no paper.'

'Well, what you doin' up there, Johnny, that not your country?' Aunty Ida waved a stick in his direction.

'My uncle, Yorta Yorta man. My country enough.'

'We need you here, Johnny,' his aunt replied.

Johnny said nothing. Uncle George had his back to all of them, mumbling amerjiyt every now and then, while he plucked the ears of the bitch who'd weasled her way inside his cloak. Amerjiyt.

Gwennie came up the beach heavily and lay down on a mat, turning her swelling belly to Alec. The kids skipped up the sand, shellfish bundled in their shirts. Errol passed two crayfish to Veronica who put them on their backs in the coals.

'Nice fish, Errol,' Veronica said.

'He never gottem, Vronica, I got 'em in the garden pool,' little Tussock bragged. They called it the garden pool because it had neptune's necklace and sea lettuce growing all about the edge and it was big enough to attract crays to shelter in its caves, waiting for the tide to bring in what it would.

'Well, doesn't matter who gottem, they're good fish,' and she took the abalone from their extravagantly proud hands and set the fish upside down in the coals to poach in their juice. The kids stared at the feast, proud that they'd contributed to it on such a day. They could smell the big tuna Johnny had caught from his canoe, steaming in its grass basket. They ate most of it last night but there was still plenty left for the funeral feast.

The billy of tea was passed around amongst them, kids and all, but Aunty Ida declined.

'Errol, you be a good boy, and get your Aunty's cup for her,' she said to her grandson who was pleased she'd asked him. That cup was precious. 'What's that Barmah country like, Johnny?'

'Real good, Aunt, we got a big island in there, right back in the forest. Catch crays an' cod. Plenny tucker, Aunt. Good country.'

'You got crays?'

'White ones. Murray crays. Chorriong. Big cod, yella belly, mussel. Ceremony.' The camp went quiet thinking of a people with ceremony. They could all see the pull of a country still with ceremony.

Gwennie eased herself, settling her belly, not too deliberately but enough for Alec to get the message. He kept his dead eye angled her way and studied his cousin, Johnny, saw where the ochre was being smudged from his face while the billy was passed and the food shared. Veronica pulled the big stone jar out of the cool sand and wiped it clean. She passed it to Uncle George who had to angle it awkwardly to sip from the spout so he didn't disturb the dog. Aunty Ida wanted to finish off her cup of tea first but the jug was passed between everybody else.

'Alec reckons we should get back to the island,' Aunty Ida said and tried to study her man's face but Uncle George said nothing. 'Reckons we should go an' see how Gavin is.' No one said anything.

'I'll go,' said Gwennie not looking up. Alec turned his good eye to her.

Silence.

The last of the shellfish were steaming on the coals, the tuna was plucked from the bone, the billy settled back in place, the jug passed, a sweet column of driftwood smoke curling slowly away from the camp across the still water of the bay. Breath, breath, breath whispered the docile waves amongst the coarse sand and broken shells.

Aunty Ida watched the faces, wondering about the scattering of the stars.

April 16, 1854. 1800 hours.

Unknown vessel. Low in the water. Labouring. Southerly passage.

Caleb put down the pen and wondered about the vessel. Trying to see it. He returned to the balcony of his tower and listened. Between the crashing of waves he could hear the creaking of ropes but not a murmur of slack from the sail. They were pushing it, had her reefed tight, plenty on board. Not fishermen, not mid strait like that, not with so many on board. Wouldn't be sealers, boat too small. Plenty in the boat. Blackfellows? Couldn't be. Where'd they get a boat?

He returned to the table and his massive log. 'She was truly beautiful,' he wrote. A ship? A woman? Yes, a woman, but a black woman. 'She had that grace which draws the eye. I'm sure I've written this before but you'll have to bear with me. A ship just passed. Small vessel. Well loaded. Made me think of Belle and her people sailing my whaleboat back and forth across the strait. I saw that boat more than once after . . . the time I took Belle back to the mainland. You'll be amused by the verb took.

'And I wonder about West. I haven't seen him since but every now and then people mention him, not because they've seen him but because they've heard of him.' He paused to pace about the small kitchen. The galley. Made tea in a pot and leant on the window ledge while it brewed. A gull, perched on the railing of the balcony, stared at his face, ducking its head to get a better perspective, made uncertain by the plunder the disease had made of his features. The bird, not sure whether it was looking at a face, confused by the craters and gulfs, was convinced to fly off and find a more wholesome perch.

The gull was right. There was something gruesome about Captain Mathews' decline. Not just that he was sick and blind but that he was so tamely allowing his life to ebb away, to leach onto a page of a log which might go unread for all he knew. When the authorities discovered he was blind they'd surely declare the log worthless, toss it in the sea, out the window and into the sea. The Captain had considered this, had even ruminated upon it in the pages of the log, a weird plea to the humanity of his fellow keepers of the light. And it may work. A man may happen upon the log who is conscious of the chaos in men's hearts but then again it might be found by one who has manacled chaos, managed chance, murdered hope, simply by relying on the ancient principle of mathematics. Time, date, event. Time, date, event. The absolute worst person to find this book would be an historian. Then the truth could never be told.

Five
BARREN

Stock watched the small craft labouring in the heavy swell. He didn't need the glass to tell him it was full of blackfellows. No one else would crowd so many into so small a boat. Taking water too by the looks. He pointed to the horizon. Chub went to the wheelhouse and observed the craft through the old telescope.

'Aunty Ida and the mob. Alec at the tiller. She's sailing low.'

'Taking water,' was Stock's only contribution.

Alec recognised the *Yolla* but couldn't steer the *Dalrymple* away from the wind and had to wait for Chub to bring his boat alongside.

'She's taking water,' he told Chub.

'Will you make the island?'

'Think so.'

'Better go down south. We'll have to slip her and see what's the trouble.'

'I don't want to take it to George Town, it's Mrs Mathews old boat. She gave it to me. I've got a paper.'

'Alright, well we'd better see if old man West might

help us. He's the only one I know can steam the boards an' such. Take the mob on to Flinders and try and sail her on to Barren. I'll follow you down an' try and find Mr West.'

'You gunna stay overnight, Chub?' Veronica asked, 'it's getting dark soon.'

'We'll take you mob on to Flinders and then I'll go across to Barren with Alec. The *Dalrymple* is nearly under. She'll be better without all this load on. That Gwennie's nearly sinkin' her.'

Gwennie blushed.

'Well you get back soon as you can, Chub, you've got a bit of marryin' to do if my memory's right.'

'Your memory's not bad, Aunt.' But Stock clucked his tongue. A prolonged spell on land by the sound of things.

With the light of a half moon the *Dalrymple* and *Yolla* picked their way carefully through the shoals of the Sound following the course old Delano had plotted in his log. Chub knew enough to do it on his own but Alec was comforted by his knowledge, proud that he'd been able to read the chart and make the harbour in Kent's Bay.

They camped on board the *Yolla*, waiting for first light, wondering where the hell they'd start looking for Aunty Woonaji and Mr West.

But they needn't have bothered. When Stock came on deck at piccaninny light an old woman was sitting on the crude jetty, waiting.

'Aunty,' Stock said, 'Aunty Woonaji?' The old woman nodded. 'We're Kennedy's, cousin a' that Hummock mob, Aunt Ida's people, Uncle Georgie Hummock. We need some help with Alec's boat. We heard Mr West knew boats like this.' Stock indicated the *Dalrymple* tethered to *Yolla*'s stern.

Chub stuck his head out of the hatch.

'This is me brother, Chub, Aunty.' The woman nodded and then stared at them a while longer before rising and walking back into the tea-tree. Chub looked at Stock.

'She wants us to wait,' Stock said.

'She didn't say nothin'.'

'She wants us to wait.' Stock repeated.

They sat on the deck and had a cup of tea while Alec told them about the voyage across the strait with Mrs Mathews.

'Old Mr West was on Captain Mathews' ship, *Ocean*.' Chub told Alec and was about to explain the whole Sea Elephant Bay operation when Woonaji reappeared and signaled for them to tow the *Dalrymple* around into a little creek at the end of Kent's Bay.

They had to tie *Yolla* up to a wattle stump and haul the wallowing *Dalrymple* on account of the shallowness of the water, but eventually they came to a small beach where an old frame and windlass had been erected. Chub noticed *Ocean*'s old whaleboat upturned on logs with half the hull stripped back ready for caulking.

And then he saw the old man.

West was sitting on a stack of sawn planks smoking a hand made pipe. West was looking at the *Dalrymple*.

'Hello, Mr West, I'm Chubber Kennedy, this is my bother, Stock, and this is Alec Hummock, Aunty Ida and Uncle George's son.' West nodded and walked over to inspect the boat.

He wasn't a tall man and he was a bit stooped in the back and his beard was snow white except where the pipe had stained it yellow on the right side. He was very old, that was plain. Woonaji settled herself on the sand and stripped lengths of messmate bark and rolled them into plaited strips on what remained of the meat of her thigh.

West indicated for the young men to attach ropes to bow and stern of *Dalrymple* while he turned the windlass, drawing the boat up a ramp of adzed logs and tipping her gently as she came so that by the time she was clear of the water she was almost on her port gunnel. Using the long levers at either end of the windlass frames they were able to tip her right over and bring her to rest upside down. This procedure had obviously been used many times over the years to repair the whaleboat without being seen from the bay.

Old West walked about the hull prodding the planks with a short bladed knife before walking off to where Woonaji was stoking the fire and boiling a billy for tea and beside it a pot of pitch for the repairs. Alec couldn't decide which pot smelt most like Aunty Ida's tea.

Woonaji left the fire from time to time to check some lines she had set beside a fallen log that extended half way across the stream. Within the space of the hour it took for old man West to finish his cup of tea and a couple of pipes his wife pulled in three large bream and a huge flathead. Alec was curled on his side by the fire, sound asleep.

Woonaji set the pitch to one side and heaped hot sand and coals around it to keep it pliable while she placed the fish in green rush baskets and set them in the coals beside a similar basket of daisy roots. West watched his wife's preparations without any discernible expression escaping the thicket of his beard. 'You've been here a long time, Uncle.' Chub commented.

'Yueh,' the old man replied unconsciously using the Bunurong word of his wife's language.

'Must be thirty years easily.'

'Forty-one.'

'Forty-one?'

'Come 'ere in, what, 1817. In the whaleboat. Captain Mathews brought us.'

'You don't miss going to sea, Uncle, the ports?'

'Nooh,' it was almost a sigh, 'nooh, this is enough for me.'

'Just you and Aunty Woonaji?'

'Nooh, nooh, few others time to time. Few others 'er mob, time to time. Live way over,' he indicated vaguely with his pipe. Woonaji glanced back at him, seeming to ensure his directions weren't too explicit.

'No one see you mob here, Uncle, you never come across to our island. All them years.'

'Oh, yes, long time you know.' He indicated his wife. 'She scared of that mission, you know.'

'But it's been closed for years.'

'Oh yes, yes, but she doan like those whitefellas, doan like them sailors. Treat her bad, treat all her people bad, you know. Even Captain Mathews, you know, he use that gun, you know.'

'Aunty Belle's mob.'

'All this mob. All that time on Sea Elephant, you know. Terrible on that island. Make you shame, you know. Treated 'em like animal, you know. An' I feel sick, real bad, an' then she tell me 'bout this place, 'bout all this place 'ere. Oh yes, yes, she tell me alright, that one. We got everythin' 'ere, you know. She tell me that.' And he stared at his wife's back as she broke up sticks with surprising energy for one so old and frail.

'Reckon we can fix the boat?'

'Ooh, yes, yes. Patch her up. Good boat. Good timber.' He nodded to himself apparently emphasising the goodness of boat and timber.

Stock had gone to sleep cradling his cup in his lap. Chub was getting sick of maintaining the whole conversation himself but Woonaji solved that by sliding some fish onto a bark sheet and topping it with a bunch of the little tubers glistening in their own juice. The three of them ate the meal while Stock and Alec snored.

A giant lilly pilly spread a dark green canopy over the grassy verge of the beach but didn't completely prevent the sun from reaching where they sat by the fire. Grey fantails flitted and farted around the foliage, dragonflies hovered over the stream and mullet leapt at them occasionally, punctuating the somnolence of the river bank with their foolish belly whackers.

'Old Captain Mathews is at the lighthouse on Deal.'

'That so. That so. Lighthouse is it?'

'He's blind now, been like that for twenty odd years.'

'That so. That so. Poor man. He bit cheeky sometime but he brought us here. Good to us two people. And his wife.'

'She died just two weeks ago.'

'That so. Oh, poor thing. Woonaji, Missus Mathews she be derdwa now.'

The old man's wife stood up from her tasks to look at Chub with her eyes glistening.

'You see that lady was good to us here. Very good. When Woonaji have baby, you know. Plenny times she send us things. Plenny times. Flash things, you know. Things for baby an' such.'

'You had a baby?'

'Oh yes, yes, long time now, long time, but he died that one, poor thing.' And the old man glanced at his wife who knelt suddenly by the fire and poked and shovelled at the coals causing skeins of smoke to plume around her. 'Oh yes, yes, that long time now, long time.'

At last the old man roused himself and crabbed his way around the hull of *Dalrymple* gouging between the planks, stripping out the old caulking and carefully rasping out the joints with the edge of a large, razor-sharp mussel shell. Woonaji joined him with the pot of pitch and together they worked at the hull pressing in the cords of plaited bark and sealing them with the simmering pitch. Systematically the two old people worked up and down the length of the hull, their hands working together as if from the one body. Chub imagined all their tasks must be like this and it struck him like the slap of a mullet full in the kisser, these two scrawny old wrecks loved each other and he watched them surreptitiously while they were absorbed in their work and saw how she was quick to flick any gob of searing pitch from his hand, while he steadied her elbow when the short woman had to reach up toward the keel of the boat to insert more bark fibre. They loved each other. They touched. A great wash of emotion surged through him and Chub determined that he'd be back at Wybalena that very night to tell Veronica what he thought about two old hands working together.

When they came back to the fire and Woonaji served the fish and tubers to Stock and Alec, who had roused themselves at last, Chub waited until old West had lit his pipe and settled the fresh cup of tea in his palm before asking him the big question.

'You must have done well from the seals, Uncle?'

'Oh yes, yes.'

'So what made up your mind to come here?'

'She tell me.'

'Aunty?'

'Oh yes, yes, she tell me 'bout this life 'ere, you know, tell me 'bout rivers an' mountains an' such. Just what I wanted, you know. Sick of that life. Those men. Sick of . . . ,' he seemed to search for the English word for his thought before giving up. 'Oh yes, yes, she told me.' And he gazed at his wife who was giving the fire a hell of a good poking. 'Oh yes, yes, plenny good life she told me. Plenny good.'

'But very quiet, Uncle.'

'Oh yes, yes, quiet alright, very quiet, oh, yes, yes.'

'And you don't miss seeing white fellas?'

Woonaji suddenly turned from her work at the fire. 'He not whitefella, he nuthin', he be born on boat.'

'Oh yes, yes,' the old man agreed, 'that's nothin' to me at all. I been all at sea.'

Chub wondered about Veronica and the life they might have, but he had to do the wondering all by himself because everybody, absolutely everybody had gone back to sleep. Two dogs slunk down to sniff around the fire, crunching at crispy bits of fish skin and potato, before curling up, one each, behind the knees of the old man and woman.

He stood beside the log inspecting the handwoven fishing lines, plaited hair and bark, noticed the steel fish hook on one, the shaved shell hook on the other and wondered which caught the most . . . or if they were for different fish. He gazed about the river bank, the slip cradle West had made, the campfire, the people sleeping beside it, the dogs opening an eye to stare at him each time he moved, the lilly pilly towering above them, the crouching shapes of tea-tree and wattle at the water's edge and he wondered at the pact between a man and a woman, this white man and this black woman and how they'd come by this . . . arrangement, this arrangement where they could live in the country with almost no one knowing that they were alive, no one to know that they were, impossibly, in love, at the far end of a spectrum on which his own family was in the middle and the white people, the real white people, were at the opposite end.

Old Man West roused himself and reached for his cup. He seemed to have the ability to make a great deal out of his pipe and cold cup of black tea, saying nothing for long stretches without ever appearing to be refusing to talk. Chub had never seen Stock sleep for more than three or four hours at a time, especially on land, but here he'd managed to sleep through most of a day.

Chub was a young man about to be married, he wanted to find out how some made it into something completely different to most of those he'd witnessed. He had to know what made West, a fellow man, tick.

'Uncle, you must have spent a lot of time with Captain Mathews?'

'Oh yes, yes, good sailor.'

'How long were you at sea?'

'All my life.'

'But where were you born?'

'On board. They told me I was born on board.'

'But what about your mother?'

'Don't know. Never knew a mother or a father. Just the ship. The *Shearwater*.'

'So what made you come here . . . with Aunty?'

'Oh, well,' once again he seemed to search his reduced English vocabulary, 'well, she told me, that one,' and he indicated his wife asleep near his feet, now with the two dogs snuggled close, 'she told me 'bout this place, the mountain an' rivers and such an' . . . well . . .' Then the old man looked quickly at Chub and did a very strange thing, he sort of gave a knowing look and pretended to twirl the end of a moustache he didn't have, and mouthed a word at Chub.

'What's that, Uncle?'

'Sss,' he whispered quietly and once again indicated the old woman.

'What you sayin' ol' fella?' she grumbled from behind a dog's haunch, 'what you tellin' 'bout?'

'Just say you good one, missus.'

'Good one eh.'

'Merrijee bagurk.'

'Too right. Merrijee alright. Alright longa you ol' man.'

Chub saw the old man's eyes glisten with cheek and . . . moisture, but nothing more was said. He used his foot to rhythmically push at the dog closest to him so that it rocked the old woman gently.

'Good 'nuff for you ol' guli man,' she mumbled and Chub saw a little crease at the corner of the old lady's mouth. 'Kanamo you ol' fella. Give you plenny kanomo.'

West's shoulders seemed to be moving as if some gentle rumble had disturbed his chest, a silent laugh. What's the secret, Chub quizzed himself, what's their bloody secret?

'Uncle, what's your real name?'

'West.'

'Yes, but your first name?'

'Oh, that, oh, they said I was Silas but that's all, they only ever called me West once I was big enough to pull on a rope.'

'Uncle, I'm getting' married.'

'Oh yes, yes.'

'To that Vronica, Alec's cousin.'

'Oh, yes.'

'Reckon it's the right thing?'

'Oh yes, yes,' he said pushing the dog again so that the old woman rocked to and fro gently. 'Oh, yes, yes.'

But there was no hope of getting back to the big island now, it was almost dark and Alec was snoring like a grampus and Stock seemed to be infected by it too. Must be something in the wood smoke.

The old man was happy just to stare out at the water, so it looked like it was up to Chub to get the next meal. Ducks had been flying up stream ever since the sun lowered against the horizon. His gun was on *Yolla* anchored well back downstream but even if he had it he'd be a mongrel to fire it with everyone still asleep. He must have clicked his tongue in annoyance but the old man pulled a big hook-ended boomerang from behind the log he sat on and pushed it to Chub with his foot and then smoothed the sand and drew a map of the river with the stem of his pipe. Upstream, maybe a hundred, two hundred yards, there must be a small shallow lake. Tolum, the old man mouthed. It was like being with Uncle George.

But sure enough not far up stream the creek opened into a reedy lake and it was covered in duck, swans and spoonbill with more arriving every minute.

Chub hurled the boomerang low across the water and it gave a solid clip to a teal before cannoning into a spoonbill and breaking its neck. Just as he was about to retrieve the boomerang and tuck the birds under his arm he saw the unmistakable glide of a flounder disturbed by his feet. He followed its dim shape as it arced stealthily away and was able to creep up to it, minimising the splash by pointing his toes as he entered and withdrew his feet from the water. He struck down with the sharpened hook of the deadly boomerang and scooped up a stunned fish as large as the top of a cream can. He had to hold it through the gills to stop it slipping out of his grip.

Stock and Alec were sitting up waiting for their tea and the dogs seemed to have been waiting impatiently, too.

No hope of getting home tonight, even if he was about to get married.

Six
BARMAH

Uncle George hadn't seen anyone ochred for a long time and when the Bunurong, his wanung, brought Johnny over to Sea Elephant Bay for the funeral he was entranced.

The silhouette of the outrigger canoe entering the bay clubbed him on the chest like a liangil, disturbed by the power of the craft's ancient curves and the hoops and bars of ochre on chest and arm. His chest hurt, his testicles moved, it was stirring the man in him, calling to his maleness, to his responsibilities for his people, and so, after the two days of the ceremony, when it was time for the Bunurong to return to the mainland, Uncle George was with them, bringing the trim of the craft perilously close to the waterline. They were a mile out to sea before Johnny noticed the tip of a tail poking out of Uncle George's possum skin. He's brought that bloody dog, no wonder we're nearly sinking.

They didn't land at Port Albert, too provocative, you never knew what the latest pretext for harassment or incarceration would be, what crime would be found to which any black man's description would match.

So the journey away from the coast avoided the little communities springing up on the best river flats and glades, kept clear of the grog shanties, wide of the isolated homesteads and the dogs trained to attack black men.

They stayed when they could with the impoverished camps on the more isolated rivers where hungry people searched for the few remaining myrniong gardens the sheep had yet to find. Johnny's party listened with faces flushed with shame while the people discussed ways in which a bag of flour might be procured, the only acceptable currency being women. A man could work for a week and earn a cup of tea and a pair of pants with the knees all gone. Cut two ton of wood for a loaf of bread with the bottom all charred, the one they were going to give to the chooks.

They mingled with the mob at mission stations and most times the missionary was none the wiser, they all looked the same to him.

And there they were scorched with further shame while the people chanted hymns and prayers and those who prayed were fed bowls of soup and stale bread. Those who didn't went without. You could turn a Muslim into a Jew with that policy. The people were starving.

Oh, there were still fish in the rivers but the chances were you'd be shot while you set the nets or have the fish stolen from you when they were full. There were kangaroos left but how could you hunt them without exposing yourself to the Christian horsemen.

Uncle George witnessed in astonishment crow men living with crow women and Ganai living with Bunurong. All these people crowded together, living together, praying together, begging together and eventually sleeping together against the law. But how could you blame them. They were hungry and the law had not protected them from the power of the amerjie.

All the more reason for Uncle George to follow

Johnny up to the Barmah. There was never a question of what Caleb would do; he did what his cousin did.

Rightly speaking it wasn't Uncle George's country. But what was right these days? He was Bunurong and this was Yorta Yorta country, but it was still country his people used to visit. Before the war.

Now his people were just as likely to be taken up in neck chains to Lake Maloga and such places. If you didn't go of your own free will, out of the freedom of your own biting hunger. But they stayed at the ruins of old missions which had dissolved simply because the Lutherans in Bonn or the Wesleyans in London got distracted and forgot to feed them. Found more exotic primitives to foster, people who perhaps wore penis gourds or lip plates, something more meaty for a Christian to get his teeth into.

But Johnny Mullagh had other ideas, a subversive plan to avoid poverty and shame.

The Barmah people had welcomed him into their community deep in the flooded forest where amerjie got lost in the maze of channels and billabongs. And Johnny had said to Uncle George, 'Plenny of your people up there too, Uncle. Taungurong, Wurrunjerri, Dantgurt, Bunurong, all people there in that forest.' He named some of the people, people related to Uncle George, Wandin mob, Bookar mob, Kneebone fellas. 'Yeah, Uncle, ol' Granny Kneebone she be askin' 'bout you, you know. "Where that Uncle George?" she say alla time, "I feed that lil' fella plenny time." That what she said, Uncle.' But Uncle George needed no convincing, he'd seen enough.

God knows how old Granny Kneebone was. No one could remember when she wasn't called Granny. Couldn't remember when her bush name was Goolwa Narbun. But did God know? Did God care? Plenty of people were wondering what kind of God could love thy bloody neighbour one minute and cast down false idols in the next! Johnny learnt much from the talk in the Barmah.

He had the arrogance of a white man. Some of the ruthlessness, too. Certainly had their contempt for the spirit of God.

They were out in the forest collecting bark sheets for the roof of the new hut they were building in the Barmah, but Uncle George needed a cup of tea so they lit a fire, or Johnny did anyway, and sat beside it looking out across the billabong.

'You see, Uncle, we gotta fight for this land now. We sit down here long enough they'll decide they want it. We steal even one bullock every now an' then, even one, that mob find out an' they come out shootin'. We gotta do somethin', Uncle, gotta find some way of keepin' this land.'

'Yueh, keepim.'

'If we just do it blackfella way we'll lose it. In the dry season, they'll come in 'ere with their horses an' when they see our huts they'll chase us off.'

'Yueh, chasim.' Johnny stared at the old man. How could he make him understand that they had to fight it like whitefellas. Fight for their land. Get it on paper.

'If we can't do it their way, they'll chase us off again and again. No matter how many times we move, set up camp.'

Uncle George was listening to his nephew. Proud of the young wanung. Good warrior that Johnny Mullagh, but chasin' tail. Johnny jabbed a stick into the fire causing the coals to break up and the sparks to fly. Can't make an angry fire, Uncle George thought, ngala wiyn bitjarra. The small birds of the forest had come to visit them. Blue wrens, pootpooteyt, skittered in the leaves and twigs, the males proud and blue, willy wagtails, yellpillup, feinted and flared on the mud of the river bank, bringing the news, spreading the story, and the tree creeper, teetayar, piped from the base of beal, the redgum, pipe, pipe, pipe, it called incessantly, come,

come, come, it was insisting, come, come, come, there is food, the small bird's throat pulsed and throbbed with the urgency of its song, the urgency to keep doing those things which would bring life.

'Teetayar,' Uncle George said, delicately indicating the bird with a twig. 'Yingally, mooron. He be callin' his mob you know, callin' all them bird, come come come he singing out, kurr kurr, kurr kurr.

'That one holdin' on to his country. Good one, that bird. Merrijee neremba.' Johnny tried to show respect for his Uncle's metaphor, for his explanation of the working of the spirits, but he'd gone past hoping the spirits would be able to assert themselves against the guns, against the hordes, against the righteousness. Uncle George sensed his nephew's impatience and frustration, you just had to look at the tension in his limbs, but he couldn't help him, in Uncle George's mind you had to have faith in the country, in the spirits of the ancestors in whatever shape they represented themselves, you had to have faith that the spirits would persist, even in the depths of your own deep sorrow, even with the knowledge that in the process your own life would be sacrificed, even in the knowledge that the secret, sacred understanding of how all the elements of the earth combined to regenerate themselves was being lost behind the hymns, behind the English, behind the boots and shirts and dresses, while all the ceremony that gave people their spirit and understanding was being beaten out of you, even while you were made to feel ashamed of lying on the earth listening to its heart beat up through you, whispering its love and secrets in your ear, even while all that was being lost, and would remain lost, even while that was happening you had to hold on to your ground, listen to the birds, watch the tree creeper's throat and see the blood of the whole universe throbbing in it, everyone's blood excited by the urgency of the call to join the celebration. That's what Uncle George thought in his language, a language which was now a secret, a deadly secret.

Oh, you could get a bit of paper, you could beg on paper to get another piece of paper, but it meant nothing, these people, these amerjie, they slaved, they flogged themselves, their horses, their wives and their children all in pursuit of the paper and then just as quickly lost interest and went somewhere else, built a new house, new fences, in country which had no connection to the land they'd just left. They'd leave the ground that was beginning to recognise them, beginning to show grudging respect for their spirit, just up and leave with never another thought for the ground they'd demanded should feed them, should shelter them. No respect. No love. No, Uncle George thought, paper no bloody good.

Johnny sulked beside him aware that all his uncle's thoughts were internal.

They gathered the bark in a heap and then caught some crayfish and cod before tying the bark to each other's backs and trudging their way along the ancient dryland path between the redgums. Hans Heysen would have been moved to paint it, except he would have painted out the colour of their skin, Tom Roberts would have turned his back on them and gone looking for a more industrious settler with a steel axe, a pipe and a more civilised air of industry.

Uncle George knew nothing about how artists might or might not represent his people but Johnny was aware of the contempt his people attracted, the scorn for their mutual humanity.

He tried to respect his uncle's spiritual determination but he'd seen people shot for their faith, he'd seen some proud, faithful, profoundly dignified men and women mocked by men who laughed at semen and shit, rejoiced in pain and humiliation. Oh, not all men, even Johnny acknowledged that, but you didn't need many, especially if deep within the intruder's heart he knew that the awful deeds of his less cultivated fellows cleared the ground for their own more scrupulous hands.

Johnny had seen a grandfather invested with all the wisdom of the thousands of generations shot stone dead by a boy of sixteen. 'I thought he was going for his spear,' the child successfully claimed. 'It was him or me.' And the adult men left the old black man there, led the white boy away with a paternal hand on his shoulder, proud that he'd taken responsibility to protect the land. Been blooded. Johnny knew that one day it could be Uncle George they'd turn over with an insolent boot in order to mock his nakedness.

Johnny felt this deeply. He could respect his uncle but could see plain as day the outcome of such a course. He felt certain that if he was to be faithful to his people he had to follow a different course. He had some of the skills, he could read, he'd sat at the feet of his surrogate mother, Eugenie Mathews and seen the way she strove to support her school in a hostile community. Useful skills, but they couldn't alter the fact that up here he didn't know any white people in positions of power who he could trust absolutely.

That's when he decided to go and see Kenna. Kenna cut fence posts and rails out of the redgum forest. He lived on his own and treated the black people well. If you asked for tea he'd give it to you, if you were hungry he'd give you bread and worry about how to replace it later. His fellow whites thought he was a simpleton because he lacked ambition, living in a rough hut on a potato sack bed, no glass in the window. But they didn't know that Kenna felt that what he had was about as much as any man deserved. Oh, he had alcohol as a companion, but many are like that without escaping God's love. The white God. Johnny suspected that Kenna would know little more than himself about the mysterious power of paper but he might know where to start, who to trust.

Kenna's eyes were going a bit crook on him so when he saw Johnny approaching along the track he moved over toward his axe, pretending that the next job he'd had in mind was to sharpen it. He might have been kind but he wasn't a complete idiot. He couldn't see the figure well enough to know whether he was black or white but it moved like a black man, almost noiseless, the feet gentle on the ground. The shirt and trousers weren't new but they were tidier than most bushmen, certainly in better nick than Kenna's own. But then he recognised Johnny and moved to kick the fire into life and then to Johnny to shake his hand.

'How're ya, Johnny? Good ta see you.'

'Good-o, Kenna. Got cup a tea?'

'Too right, mate, too right I have, bit of damper here too. Not as good as that Granny Kneebone's but good enough toasted up a bit.' Kenna was truly pleased. Two mates could sit by the fire and have their tea and damper, bit of a smoke, a chin wag, the redgum could wait.

Johnny watched while his friend knocked the coals together and set the billy boiling almost straight away. Built a fire like a black man he did, no great showy blaze, just a few sticks and a good set of coals, always a bit of heat below.

After the plain meal of stale, toasted damper, Kenna shared his tobacco, pleased as punch just to have someone companionable to share it, someone not so uppity to laugh at Kenna's manners or his torn pants.

'Kenna, our mob bin buildin' camp back in bush.'

'Oh, I know that. I see ol' Granny an' the kids fishin' for crays on the river. She told me that. While you was away I had a lend of Fletcher's cart to carry the posts an' so forth an' on the way back I took out some loose iron an' bags. Oh, yes, I seen that camp, nice little place out there, nice an' dry all year round out there.'

'You got paper for your place, Kenna?'

'Paper?'

'You know, title, own it?'

'Ohh, no, no, not me. Never even thought of that, Johnny, I just keep movin' to 'nother stand of timber . . . wherever they tell me to start cuttin' next.'

'Well what about the squatters, what they got?'

'Don't know. Don't say I know what they got. They'd have somethin'. Yes, they'd have to have somethin'.' Kenna thought for a while, made as if having trouble with his smoke, pulling shreds of tobacco from the end while he wondered about the direction of his friend's interest. Maybe the policeman Foxy Ferguson would know, he thought, but then dismissed it, no decent Irishman involved the police unnecessarily. 'I could ask Fletcher, I suppose, he's pretty well set up out there, house and such he's got, he'd have to have somethin'.'

'What that fella like?'

'Like? Oh not a bad sort, I suppose, not a bad man, pays up, don't grizzle about little things. Let's me be. Yes, let me have his cart that time, let me use it to bring back a few of me own things. Like the time I got the tin for Granny.'

'Could you ask him 'bout the paper?'

'Oh yes, sure I could.'

'And not say it was for us mob.'

'Oh . . . oh, oh I see. Oh yes, I'll say like I'm thinkin' of buyin' me own place. He might believe that. Yes, he might. I'll ask him, Johnny.'

And they finished their smokes like that, in a kind of wondering and slightly troubled silence.

A few days later Johnny was coming back along the camp road with some fish when he came across Kenna and Uncle George sharing a bottle by the river.

They were watching a pair of pardalotes making a nest in the pipe of a broken redgum branch. They didn't say a lot, just passed the bottle companionably and signalled for Johnny to join them. He waited for Uncle George to nod before he sat down.

'How you goin', Johnny?'

'Good-o, Kenna.'

'I saw old Fletcher about that paper business, you know. Seems you gotta go to the Lands Office in Echuca, they're divvyin' up the land from there. Got blocks drawn up all up an' down the river. Says I'd have no trouble gettin' one.'

'What about us?'

'Don't know, ol' Fletcher never mentioned that.'

The three sat in silence for a while as the male bird came back and entered the little wooden tunnel. Parrots piped their clear bell notes across the water, crows cawed mournfully from the sand ridges.

'Would you ask, Kenna? For us mob. Ask about this bit here?'

'Oh, sure, Johnny, yeah, course I could. Do it next week. Yeah, that'll be right.'

And he did as he said he would. Kenna was like that. But crikey he felt uncomfortable asking. The Lands' bloke wore a tie and shoes, real shoes, not boots, and he looked at Kenna as if he was a tramp. Decided to humour Kenna. Not that Kenna didn't notice but he didn't have the words or temerity to complain.

'And what piece of land did you have in mind, Mr ... er ...'

'Kennedy.'

'Ah yes, Mr Kennedy. And your occupation Mr Kennedy.'

'Timber cutter.'

'Timber cutter, of course.'

That's how the conversation went but Kenna had to cop it. Thing is, he could read a map as well as anyone and saw immediately the piece that the Yorta Yorta were camped on.

'Well what about this bit then, how much is that?'

'Oh that, Mr Kennedy, that floods, very low land, that's a Crown Reserve.'

'What's Reserve mean?'

'Well, Reserve is, well it's held in reserve for graziers and the like.'

'So, I could graze it?'

'But you said you were a timber cutter.'

'But I might get some bullocks, to cart me wood.'

'Oh, well we'd have to see about that. But you can't buy Crown Reserve, you understand, it's for the use of the Crown.'

Even Kenna knew that this information was no more use to Johnny's mob than if they'd said no outright. It seemed you could use it but there'd be no paper, if there was paper it belonged to the Crown. Kenna knew that meant the King but what the King wanted with a redgum swamp he was buggered if he knew.

Johnny had begun preparing the camp for his line of thinking but they got sulky and gloomy about having to approach any white person about asking for paper. Kenna's news cheered them no end. So, they wouldn't have to apply for paper after all, couldn't if they wanted to. Just had to go about things as they'd been doing. The King'd never find out.

They were happy enough, but Johnny knew that a day would come when the King would discover that he had a desperate purpose for that very same bit of swamp even though he'd never seen it, and if things went well with the throne, would never have to see it. He'd rather visit the Tower than Australia in any case. In the minds of most Englishmen they were much the same thing.

So the Barmah camp developed an economy of cod, crayfish and redgum. They could live off the river and its lagoons, they knew the farmers' wives they could approach to sell fish and firewood, and with the cash they could buy their tea, sugar and flour, even the occasional bottle. Sometimes they'd work for Kenna building a fence for a farmer who didn't object to having blackfellows on his property.

It was generally peaceful in the forest. Oh, the grog would get the better of someone every now and then but these weren't mission people, they were workers, too proud to bend the knee to the church. The police would come across one of their children every now and then and drag them off to Lake Maloga Mission for their own good but more often than not they could sneak up and recover them, secluding them once again in their forest fastness.

Uncle George was happy for a time, surrounded by so many blackfellows, but he was a sea person really, all this still water and vast spreading trees was not his place. But everybody, all his people, were making adjustments within the new constraints. The old man could appreciate his nephew's energy and determination, could see the benefits for all the people but it was really a poor blackfellows' life. They were locked in the Barmah just as his family had, to a lesser extent, been locked on their island.

Johnny's vision of a blackfellow town was gradually being realised but more and more Uncle George wanted to hear the sea, more and more he wanted to hear Aunty Ida bossing everybody around, hammering together her crude economy with her own willpower. Barmah was not much different to Wybalena in that respect except this country was not his. You could visit the forest, as his people had always done, but the journey back to the coast would be joyous with their songs of the sea. Oh, how he missed hearing those voices, hearing the animals called by their correct names, hearing the sea revered in words which had been fashioned by tongues who loved her, oh my korraiyn, oh warre-a warre-a korraiyn. Uncle George dreamt of the smell of salty air, of tea-tree groves and the pound of sea on rock.

But here, the pound was the sound of hammers as the forest men extended the yards they'd built for the wild bullocks rounded up on horseback, the heeler-dingo dogs racing in and out the redgum saplings barking with the joy and purpose of it all.

No bulgana for Wallert though, she retreated to Uncle George's possum skin and slipped her muzzle under the old man's hand and shared his dream of the seas. Sick for home as dogs always are.

The wild forest cattle were from mobs chased into the forest by the Yorta Yorta tribesman years ago when the overlanders were trying to swim them across the river. Too easy for a band of blackfellows to cut out a mob of cows with calf and make themselves merry with a whole bullock roasted in the mound ovens.

Merry for a time, because it was a mistake to steal a bullock. They cost money. Convict shepherds and drovers were tuppence a dozen but a bullock cost £15, losses like that could really sting a rich man.

That's when the war started.

And even now the squatters considered the herd, begun with those first stolen cattle, to be their own property.

News of the Barmah stockyards made white fellows envious. What was a blackfella doing with a herd of cattle, three hundred strong? They'd get that upstart Johnny Mullagh, too big for his boots that one. Get rid of all of them, too dangerous letting them build up their numbers in the forest like that. But maybe it'd be better to wait until the summer when all the cattle were yarded. News was that the niggers were using their own branding irons. Acting as if the cattle were their property. We'll show 'em who's boss!

But a lot of it was just talk over mugs of beer in the pubs. A dozen old cattlemen in a haze of pipe smoke and conviviality joshing and wise cracking and eventually turning their talk to the nuisance of having a mob of blackfellas threatening their command of the forest grazing.

Are these bad blokes? Have a look at them. Arms sinewy with hard work, the hair on them blonded from the sun, faces ruddy with it too, hugely capable men, hard workers, friendly as you like, generous as the day is long, Australians in the making, egalitarian, no one was better than anyone else, a man who didn't bend his back for his bread wasn't a man at all, free men, they were free men and having family experience of chains and lash they cleaved to freedom with a pride that burnt furnace fierce. And their respect for each other's strength and independence was expressed with heart bursting pride, 'You're a real white man, you're a mate, an Aussie mate.' They hated politicians because they got fat on their labours, they hated the English because the poms thought themselves superior because they rode horses as if they were doing dressage, not galloping helter skelter between the trees, the hat blown back from their brows, driving the horses into a reckless lather to turn the lead bullock before it made for freedom. No, the English were soft, Australians were hard, others might be richer, better educated, better dressed, better manners, but none were better men. They were currency lads, native born, this was their country and they would shape it as a paradise for hardworking men and women.

But sometimes in the forest they'd catch a glimpse of other men. Men who hated them. Resented their presence, the huge labour with which they'd hewn the redgum to make their houses, the fences which surrounded their sheep and cattle runs the size of Kent. You had to turn a blind eye to those other men who threatened the noble idea of yourself. The eye might be blind but the ear hears the forest whisper, that infuriating mosquito whine reminding you of the others' presence.

You could grumble in the pub, glance at those others from under your lowered brow but even though the whining could drive you to distraction, most of the time you could ignore it and return your thoughts and energy to the building, the building of the nation. Not just your farm and its yards and sheds but the school, the church, the district hall where all the celebrations could be shaped to the declaration of your freedom and the honour of your work.

Most were like that, but not all. Some were infuriated by the skirr of mosquitoes beside their ear on the hot summer nights. Some men were jealous. Some men were violent and cruel. Some men were jealous and violent and cruel.

The great spreading branches of the redgums dipped and reached out across the flood plains where the spring grasses were now drying and golden. Kingfishers called in the trees, cuckoo shrike voices skirled, rolling and bubbling, the hot forest air pungent with eucalypt exhalation and drying mud.

Huge red and white cattle trudged through the trees their wide horned heads swaying and nodding with their tired gait, eyes still rolling and flaring white at the dogs who barked and feinted at their legs, but too weary now to alter their gait or even strike backwards with a hoof.

These few were the last to be yarded by the Barmah people in readiness for branding with the letter Y in a circle, their own brand, their forest brand. Dust rose above the yards as the feet of two hundred cattle stamped and stirred. Sunlight shafted obliquely through the trees as in a cathedral, a cathedral where horses snort, dogs bark, whips crack and children laugh, swinging their legs on the top rail of the stalls.

Granny Kneebone wouldn't miss this for quids. All the noise, all the excitement. She's got a kero tin on the fire and she's baling out mugs of tea for the men as fast as she can go. Caleb Mathews flops down on the wheat bag he uses as a saddle and wonders what kind of a life this is for a man of the coast, but he's proud none the less. As proud as those other men, those wiry, sunburnt men in the pub, proud of his labour, proud that he can provide for his people, but unlike those other men, proud to ride beside his cousin Johnny Mullagh.

For two days the smell of singed hair and hide hung in the forest as the brand seared and spat, but gradually the dust settled as cows, weary of the business and hungry after two days in the trampled yards, hung their heads and stared between the rails of their captivity.

Little Vera Adpin saw them first while she was digging for mussels in the river. She slipped between the reeds and dumped the shellfish she'd been carrying in the hem of her skirt and ran on flashing legs to the stockyards to break the news of the white men riding.

'How many, Vera?' Granny Kneebone asked the little girl.

'Big mob,' the little girl gasped, 'big mob whitefellas.'

The men sat up from where they'd been dozing by the fire and looked toward Johnny. He'd know what to do. Johnny felt their eyes upon him and stood up slowly trying for an air of authority as well as an appearance of calm, trying to buy some time to think.

They're our cattle, he thought, got our brands now, never been yarded before them bulgana, they're ours. But in the back of his mind he had mosquito noises, too. When had the amerjie ever let them have anything? In those early years when the sheep had destroyed all the myrniong and water cress and the black fellows were starving, the white fella had been outraged by the loss of even two or three sheep. Had hunted them down for the sake of a scrawny wether.

But he went to face the amerjie wishing he hadn't

turned the horses out onto the river banks, regretting that he'd have to look up into the faces of the riders.

He recognised the constable, John Foxy Ferguson, his deputy, and a dozen, no fifteen, seventeen others, hard men, their rifles holstered to their saddles.

The riders came to where Johnny Mullagh stood and waited while their animals coughed and snorted and the chimes of stirrup and bridle rings stilled. The horses stamped and tossed their heads, it'd been a long ride through the forest.

'Whose cattle are these, Mullagh?' Foxy Ferguson asked at last.

'Wild fella, boss,' Johnny answered, ashamed of the deference that came automatically to his voice.

'Wild?'

'Forest fella, all longa river, boss.'

'Look like overland cattle to me, Mullagh. I see the brand isn't registered. That's an offence in itself. Get your niggers to turn 'em out, I'm taking possession of this mob for the Crown.'

'Wild fella, boss. We find him all longa river. Never yarded, boss, wild fella.'

'Turn 'em out.'

Johnny stood his ground unbelieving that after all the work they could be taken from him as easily as this. Anxious about his pride, too, realising how this would make him look in front of his people, what it would mean for the Barmah.

The mob at the yards saw Johnny's hesitation, saw his momentary refusal of the white man's order and slid themselves between the rails to take up whatever weapon they could find. Caleb was still sitting on his horse blanket beside the halters the men had made from bark and the bits of rope they could scrounge from the farms. There were two rifles amongst the tack and he stood up, bringing himself into proximity with the weapons as he did so.

'Alright, Carter, draw that rail,' the constable said pushing his horse forward as he spoke, the animal's shoulder bumping Johnny out of the way.

Carter leant out of his saddle and began to draw the bush pole from its mortise. Caleb couldn't think why he took up the gun, whether it was because of what those cattle represented to his people or the humiliation it would mean for his cousin, but whichever the thought, he'd taken up the weapon before he'd finished thinking it and shot Carter out of his saddle.

From that point on everybody had a different perspective of the events because the cattle leapt over the remaining rail, Carter's horse struck at the air with its hooves, all the other horses spun and weaved trying to find space between the stampeding cattle and alarmed by the rifle fire coming from the riders in their saddles.

The dust that had settled rose again in a great pall and the forest clearing was one great mill of cattle, horses and people all heading for what they thought the safest quarter and all of them choosing a different course.

Johnny could hear the crack of weapons around him but his greatest concern was to avoid the great wide horns of the cattle and their plunging feet.

In the mill of dust and animals he glimpsed women and children and other men appearing and disappearing in veils of dust, at one stage he saw a small boy beneath a horse, clinging to the stirrup leathers as the animal spun about trying to find a path between the menacing spans of horns.

The cattle were soon gone but still the rifles cracked while the tower of dust hung all about in a pall so dense you couldn't see but a few feet from you. After a while the guns were silent and all that could be heard was the distant drumming of the stampeding cattle and a gurgle like somebody choking.

But it wasn't Carter, he was dead as a stone. The party of white men returned to the clearing and lifted the dead man onto his horse, tied him there before remounting and leaving the clearing, arms at the ready, making sure that they couldn't be surprised by another attack.

But there was never any danger of that. Those who had managed to swing themselves into the low branches of the river gums climbed down now, some still carrying the clubs or branding irons they'd grabbed instinctively. Others emerged from the lagoon where they'd taken shelter in the reeds, emerging into the silent forest, silent but for the ugly gurgling in someone's throat.

All the while Johnny remained standing where he'd stood throughout the commotion, unable to move anywhere but to flinch away from horse or beast as it bore down on him. But even from where he stood now in the returned quiet he could see the body of his cousin with the back of his head torn away and almost at his feet a small boy shot through the chest and trampled by hooves, the same boy perhaps who had clung so desperately to the stirrup leathers. And further off amongst the trees he could hear the shocking, grieving wails mounting from several different directions, enough to let him know that the Barmah haven was no more, that the attempt at reclamation had been snuffed out like a poor man's candle by the thumb and forefinger of God. Would God really do such a thing, do you think? I don't know, sir, I'm only telling you what Johnny thought and he thought . . . he thought he may as well be dead and all his people with him.

Seven
FAIR DEAL

Johnny's return to the coast with Uncle George was at the time of late summer when the ocean is flattened by the hot iron of the north wind, an almost brassy sheen to the surface at noon.

They returned as beaten men. Uncle George a little rejuvenated by the sea, but Johnny too dispirited to find much solace in anything but motion.

And Uncle George did his disappearing trick, up into the mangroves to find his people, not even telling Johnny if he'd be going back to the islands. Johnny had a shot at his plan, now it was Uncle's plan and he planned never to set eyes on another white man.

So Johnny hung about the wharf at Port Albert as anonymous as any black man. Each morning for a week or two he checked the boats moored in the harbour looking for a familiar ship or even a familiar face. Maybe the Kennedy boys would be coming to sell fish, but day after day that hope dimmed. The local people let Johnny camp with them, well, he was a cousin, of course they would welcome him, but they smelt danger and trouble about him, sensed a shadow glooming above the young warrior dressed in the ludicrous cast-offs of the whites, as crazy as the rest of them, huddled in their tin shanties waiting for scraps, waiting for anything, something or nothing.

But one morning Johnny's eyes passed over a boat so small he'd dismissed it initially, but his eye returned to the name on the stern, *Dalrymple*. Johnny could read a bit, not words as difficult as *Dalrymple*, but he simply recognised the craft from his days at the Tamar school. Then he saw the form of a man sleeping under a canvas sheet between the thwarts.

He slipped into the water and swam quietly to the boat hoping that no early rising sailors would be about. He slipped his hands on to the gunnel and lifted his face to look at the man asleep in the boat. Except he wasn't asleep anymore but pointing a gaff at Johnny's face.

'Alec, it's me, Johnny Mullagh.'

'Johnny! Scared the shit outa me, thought you was punyip come to get me. What you doin' here?'

'Goin' across to see ol' Mathews. Caleb got killed. Big fight up in the river.'

'Caleb?'

'Gotta tell ol' Mathews.'

'Why?'

'Dunno, toweel, you gunna give us a lift?'

''Course.'

Alec smiled at his cousin who still had water dripping out of his hair. Johnny didn't smile back and Alec turned away to prepare the boat for the voyage.

'Where's Uncle George?'

'Up in them mangroves, where you had boat last time. Says he goin' back to his land later.'

Alec glanced at his cousin's face from time to time but didn't like the look of its expression. There was a terrible coldness there and Alec wasn't sure that he wanted to hear the full story of the Barmah troubles.

So once again the *Dalrymple* set her sails for another

Strait crossing, her canvas sheets washed with apricot and rose.

And in the stone tower the Captain wrote.

Are we born blind, or do we become sightless with our own selfishness, our determination to wrest our living from the world at the expense of all others? Does the urge to survive make us blind to our brother's fate?

I am blind and now almost without face and I look back at all that I have taken from the world and wonder in whose name did I make that claim and to what end? And in what state? Or statelessness?

Alright it has come to this. We left because we betrayed the soil. My brothers and I. My father, Eugenie's father. All. We saw, or thought we saw, that the war was lost and decided, or our fathers did, to deal with the victor in order to find for the family, to put food on the table, peace at the door. Amongst all my other crimes perhaps this was the worst, to favour our mouths and bellies over all others. I can see that room even now. Our father and Eugenie's sitting at the table with the uniformed man. And we, the sons, stood behind them guarding the door. And it was done. Our fate was sealed at that bare kitchen table cleared of all domestic clutter, anything betoken of comfort and peace.

But all of it for nought. The two men shot dead by the patriots and the children fleeing for their lives to strange quarters of the globe. Eugenie to Skomer and then with me to our Sea Elephant where with cane furniture from Canton purchased with the riches of sea furs and salvaged gold we sought to begin again, to corral a remote corner of the globe where we might bless ourselves in its blessed waters and wash away all sin. But sin came with us. We were the sin. When has it been any different? With this type of animal can it ever be any different?

Captain Caleb Mathews pushed his chair back from the table and rested his hands either side of the log book. The room's circumference of whitewashed stone seemed to breathe in time with the old man in the ancient captain's jacket, his eyes sightless, his face eroded like a fallen asteroid, burnt, cratered, expressionless.

The two cousins sailed in silence towards the tower, their eyes irresistibly drawn to the fine white column and they watched as a seabird plunged from the balcony rail to the moil of surf at its root.

'What was that?' Johnny asked his cousin.

'Gannet?'

'Went down like a stone,' Johnny replied, doubting. They sailed in closer to the island.

'Put me ashore,' Johnny said.

'What if he's not there anymore. It'd be a waste of time,' Alec argued, the plunge of the seabird making him afraid for his cousin.

'I'll go ashore anyway. Come back in a week or so. Month mebe.'

'What if there's no food there . . . you know what Chub says about that place, one chair, one cup, hard tucker.'

'I'll be right. That Caleb got no one but us and the old Captain. He should know about the Barmah.'

Johnnny swung himself onto the ladder fixed to the crude landing platform bolted to the Deal Island cliff. Alec had to wrestle the tackle and canvas to get *Dalrymple* to stand away from the piles of the platform and by the time he'd turned her out to sea he looked back to see his cousin climbing the switchback track to the top of the cliff.

Alec cooeed to his cousin. Johnny turned and raised a hand.

'Be back in a week,' Alec yelled. Johnny's hand waved uncertainly. 'Or thereabouts. I'm getting married.'

Johnny had already turned to the task of negotiating the rock path slippery with spray and the *Dalrymple* was now half a mile out to sea and all Johnny could hear was the clash of wave against cliff and gull against wind. Even so his cousin was still standing in the stern with hands cupped to his mouth.

'I'm gunna have a baby. Be a father. I'm gunna be a father, Johnny, me an' Gwennie. We're gunna call him Johnny.' Although they'd never discussed any such thing. But what did it matter there were only gannets to hear and they knew next to nothing, hard to concentrate on much when all you do for a living is dive into the sea from a height of one hundred feet, names were a bit fussy to concern feathered sea bullets.

'Yeah, we're gunna call him Johnny,' Alec yelled to his cousin. 'Gunna get married. Me an' Gwennie. Gwen. Yeah, me an' Gwen.' He stood in the stern riding the roll of the sea through the boards of *Dalrymple* still staring to where his cousin had diappeared from view, but more interested in tasting the sound of his own destiny on his tongue. 'Me an' Gwen, me wife, gunna have a baby. Bopup. Gunna root her when I get home. Try to anyway.' Not certain of the logistics of pre-partum sex. 'Me an' Gwen. Gwennie.' Still debating what he liked the sound of best, but suddenly silenced by the memory of waking beside her in the coarse grassed tussocks. The sun still warm on their skin and her nipple still turned toward his mouth like a mouse tasting the air. He leant and smelt her neck. Soap. Velvet soap. His wife uses soap, real soap, not mutton bird fat. He was impressed.

He tasted the nipple and her pelvis pressed against his thigh, hot like bread, moist like dough, and her sleeping lips parted on his neck, her hair falling across his face. And he smelt that too. Velvet soap. Beautiful. 'Me an' Gwennie,' he said, 'Gwen. Me an' me wife Gwen.' And she didn't even mind about me bung eye. 'Gwennie, my Gwen,' and tears erupted from both his eyes, good and bad.

Johnny had no such comfort, nothing soft to look forward to, no solace to be found in the fecund optimism of a woman's soft body. No, Johnny was on his own, doing his duty as always.

The tower was empty, the log shut neatly, pen on top. As he expected to find it. He made himself a cup of tea and ate one of the hard ship's biscuits, not bad dunked in tea, but only any good for crushing quartz otherwise. He was in no hurry, no hurry to find what had happened to the old captain. Didn't even bother to turn the log to the last page. Just sucked at the biscuit and stared out to the mean little peaks of the Strait.

At last he descended the stairs and walked about amongst the tussocks and yolla burrows. Inspected the Captain's little spring, the neat little weir he'd made, the garden of geraniums he'd planted around it to protect the surface from the salt laden wind. Found the vegie garden behind a wall of stone, saw that as well as the runty lettuces the captain had encouraged warrigal cabbage to colonise the stone wall, blackfellas' tucker. So, the silly old bugger had enough sense to eat some greens.

Walking around the north-eastern shore he found the rock ledge where Caleb fished. Inspected the line wound on to a neat wooden reel. Tossed out the line and watched it spin off the polished spool. Clever. A sweep bit immediately and Johnny hauled it up to the ledge and felt the fatness of its back. Nice. Eat that later, but first things first. Better get on with it.

Continued walking around the island, the crenellated bays, the upward slanting track perilously close to the sheer western face and then down to the gutter on the southern shore, immediately below the light. Knew that he could have saved himself the walk by coming here first.

Descended the steep incline between the berry bushes and tea-tree, crawling on his hands and knees beneath the low interlaced branches and came out at last above a pebbly beach. Saw the crayfish first, the

Captain's new friends, tidying him up a bit, getting rid of the loose bits, a more presentable captain. Good housekeepers crayfish, very neat.

Johnny stared down at the Captain's back, garlanded by bubble weed in the pool where he'd fallen, and now attended by his friends the undertakers.

'Caleb's dead,' Johnny called down to the captain who neither waved nor replied, just joggled a little as the sea pressed in to the bay and a surge disturbed the surface of the captain's pool. 'It wasn't my fault, Uncle, not really. We weren't doin' them any harm. They were our cattle as much as anyone's.'

But it was silly, an indulgence to talk to the captain like this, he was never going to absolve or placate, challenge or blame. So, Johnny went to sleep instead. Not like Alec with his face pressed against a young woman's perfect breast, pleasantly warmed by the sun and the urgency of her own heat. No, Johnny just had the weak autumn sun itself and a bed of coarse tussock, the screams of shearwaters frantically feeding before joining the migration north.

He didn't sleep long, an hour at best, but it wasn't too bad, having a rest, no decisions to make, fish for tea. He rose on an elbow and looked down to the captain. Still asleep in the pool. Still surrounded by his mates, fiddling in his pockets, down his shirt, up his trouser leg. Intimate mates to be sure, but not mean, not hating the captain, just tidying, straightening things out a bit. Mortuary fish, a peculiar way with autopsy.

Johnny, didn't find it hard, waiting, nothing to do, no civilisations to save. Kept up the log. Saw the *John Franklin* go by, boats he didn't recognise, entering the time, date, sea conditions.

And one day saw *Dalrymple* returning, a man and woman aboard, probably the bride, Gwennie. But he was in no hurry, waited in the tower for Alec to climb the stairs.

'Nyurra wurryn, wanung,' Alec greeted him.

'Wanung,' Johnny replied, 'cup of tea?'

'No, no, Aunty Ida says you've gotta come home.'

'Home?'

'The island.'

'I'm doin' the captain's log.'

'Johnny, if you don't come back to the island she's gunna climb that ladder and gaff ya.'

'She in the boat.'

'Too right. An' she says you've gotta come home coz she's ya mother.'

'Haven't got a mother.'

'She'll gaff ya, Johnny, she's as mad as a meataxe about getting you off this island. Said she'd gaff me if I came back without you. Says she's your mother now and yev gotta come home. Says fa you an' me to do the couta an' crays out of the *Dalrymple*. Fixed it up with Mrs Kennedy to sell the fish in George Town.'

'She's been busy.'

'Come on, Johnny, you know what she's like, an' it's no good for you here, wanung, this place no good now, no good for kin kin bil.'

'Got it all organised.'

'Look, Johnny, have a look. What you doin' this for? Young Caleb? The captain? That's no good, not gunna help no one. Come home, Johnny. We need help. I'm writin' letters to the guvman.'

'Letters?'

'Law stuff. Get paper for our island.'

'Paper?'

'Don't turn your nose up, it's not the Barmah here, this is your country, this country knows you, and we were given our island.'

'Gubba don't give. Prisons, mission, but they don't give.'

'It's not right for you to stay here, Johnny, not good.'

'You there, Johnny,' Aunty Ida's voice bellowed up from the stairwell.'

'See, I told you, she climbed the ladder.'

'Johnny,' the old lady yelled, 'you get down here

when ya mother says. This is no good for a blackfella, alright fa gubbas to rot away, but our people don't die alone, now you come down here.'

Johnny sat for a bit, looked at the open log, out the window to the sea, back to the single cup, the single chair, back to his cousin who was looking at him, eyebrows raised.

Well, I suppose they're right, not much of a life for a blackfella, even a misery guts like me.

So, he climbed down the stairs with his cousin, got grappled by his mother, kissed square on the chops by that powerful woman.

'Just a minute,' he said, and ran off along the cliff track and came back with the captain's fishing reel. 'Might come in handy.' Alec glanced at his cousin, wondering if he was pulling his leg, whether he was serious about fishing out of the *Dalrymple*, writing letters. Who could tell with Johnny?

They clambered down the cliff path and helped Aunty Ida into the boat and settled themselves before Alec set the sail and steered away from the island.

Johnny waited for the sail to fill and for the boat to turn south but she didn't.

'We're going north,' he said to Alec.

'Aunty Ida's going to get Uncle George.'

'I'm bringin' him back to the island, country or no country, there's nothin' to be gained by that silly ol' possum dyin' on his own. There's enough people been doin' that.'

So Johnny and Alec settled in for the long haul, victim of their mother's gigantic will, prepared to listen to a dozen long-winded yarns before sleep would shut her up. But sea sickness got her first.

She was terrible sensitive to the roll of the boat, began to spew almost immediately, hardly had time to begin the story about when Captain Scott's cat got tangled in the anchor chain. Alec had heard it anyway. Cat survived but hated to hear anything go clink.

The two young men watched the old lady retch

over the gunnel. Moonbirds feinted at the lumpy bits before thinking better of it. They knew it was already sufficiently undignified for the old warrior. Like them she was scouring the Strait to bring her people back together. The birds were massing to fly north to their Siberian home but Aunty Ida was in the process of collecting family to take them south. Prepared to cascade her guts into the sea if it could bring her people back to life. Would have been easier to stay home. And she loved home, loved her fire and chair, but here she was regurgitating for the entertainment of man and beast.

'You boys got anythin' better to do than stare at ol' lady bein' sick? No shipping reports to write, Johnny?'

'Johnny's gunna help me with the letters, Aunt.'

'That so,' she replied, wiping her mouth. 'Well mebe that not a bad thing. What you think, Johnny, guvmen give us our island?'

They give nothin', Johnny thought, but in deference to Alec's serious enthusiasm and his face still flushed by innocent thoughts of a young girl's breast, he said, 'Might, yeah they might, word it properly they might.'

Alec was pleased as Punch but his great-grandchildren would be dead ten years before gubba men gave even a skerrick of that land back. But at least the woman they handed the paper to was called Aunty Ida. That's something, I suppose.

A light shone golden in one of the rooms. A low room, the walls made of stone, but it's too dark to see what makes the roof. A lamp spills a buttery, tallowy light. Wispy shreds of down float in air almost tangibly greasy. Seven people are squatting in the room, bent over birds they are plucking. If you could watch them for a period of time, you would hear a companionable conversation, occasional laughter, the slap of naked birds in the enamel basin, the rounds of songs broken by curses as one singer or another coughs on a shred of flock, you'd hear argument and derisive laughter, you'd hear the scretch of quills torn from flesh, but above all you'd smell the oil and see the slippery butter-light.

And today you'd hear unusually attenuated silences. Not the sound of triumph, but the indrawn breath of survival.

ACKNOWLEDGMENTS

Aunty Ida West for many stories, Bruce Sims for insightful editing of four novels, Antoinette Smith for books and stories, Noeleen Curry for sharp reading, Sharnthi Krishna-Pillay for language editing, families of Flinders Island for books and stories, Reg Murray for stories, Lyn Harwood for stories and patience, the Australia Council for relief, Victorian Aboriginal Corporation for Languages for giving me the key to the library, John Howard for nothing, King Island for growing me up, and Blanket Bay for its waters and whispers.

The speech by Mr Hull on page 69 can be found in the Senate Papers of the Select Committee's Investigation into The Aborigines 1858–59, Victoria. Items of evidence 180, 181.

Part of the log of Amaso Delano published by Cat and Fiddle Press, Tasmania as a facsimile edition in 1973 as: *A Narrative of a Voyage to New Holland and Van Diemen's Land*

Most of the described incidents in this book did happen but not always where *Ocean* says they happened or how they happened. Geographers will find I've gently skewed the placement of islands, meddled with the elasticity of time a little, changed names, gender, generally played merry hell as novelists do, not for their own entertainment, but for the sake of the story and the grieving.

FAMILIES OF THE *OCEAN*

Crew of the *Ocean*

Caleb Mathews, captain
Silas West, crew
Vanderlin, crew
Briggs, crew
Gavez, cook
Armstrong, crew
Fanny, captured Bunurong slave
Woonaji, captured Bunurong slave and later West's wife
  on Barren Island.
Belle, captured Bunurong slave and Caleb junior's
  mother
Queen Trugannini, in a party which attacked and killed
  sealers in early days

Tamar School

Eugenie Mathews, headmistress and Cpt. Mathews'
  wife
Mrs Violet Kennedy, housekeeper

Dilly Mullagh, servant and Johnny Mullagh's mother
Johnny Mullagh, student
Bung Eye Armstrong, Johnny's uncle, uncle George's father
Hamish Black, settler killed on the Tamar
Caleb Mathews jnr, Belle's grandson
William Hull, businessman of George Town
Borthwick, owner of scouring mill
Perc Whittaker, idiot and lecher

Wybalena

Aunty Ida Armstrong
Uncle Georgie Hummock, Ida's husband
Veronica, niece to Aunty Ida
Alec Hummock, son to Ida and George
Gavin Hummock, brother to Alec
Gwennie, great niece of Queen Trugannini and wife to be of Alec
Chub Kennedy, husband to be of Veronica and captain of *Yolla*
Stock Kennedy, brother to Chub
Gracie Gardiner, niece to Aunty Ida
Ellie Gardiner, niece to Aunty Ida
Errol Hummock, nephew or close to it, of Aunty Ida
Bubby Hummock, Aunty Ida's grand-daughter
Captain Scott, white captain of strait's trader, *Argonaut*
Billy, Uncle Bungey found him somewhere
Captain Bowman, captain of the *Prion*
Karborer, Bunurong elder who helps prepare Eugenie for burial

Barmah

Granny Kneebone, Goolwa Narbun, ancient of the forest
Vera Adpin, niece to Granny Kneebone
John (Foxy) Ferguson, policeman
Kenna, forest worker
Carter, vigilante shot by Caleb jnr.

GLOSSARY

Wathaurong Language

amerjie, amerjiyt – white man
baab – breast
bagurk – woman
beal – redgum
bil – with
bilma – my
bitjarra – fight
bobup, bopup – baby
brinbeal – rainbow
bub – young person (colloquial)
bulgana – cattle
chorriong – crayfish, freshwater
cora – sand
dalang – rug
derdwa – dead
dilp – round
gammin – pulling the leg (colloquial)
geram – pigmy possum

gubba – white man (colloquial)
guli – man or male genitals
gurrk – blood
kadak – snake, large
kanamo – love
kin kin bil – blackfellows
kulkurn guli – boy
kumba – sleep
kunyaba – good
kurr kurr – come
kurrman (koorman) – seal
kutja – food
liangil – fighting club
meera (mirr) – sun (eye)
merrijee (merrijig) – good
mirrouk – spirit
mooron – alive
mum burre – sit down
murnnatja – bare
mutjaka – take
myrniong – yam cultivated by Aboriginal people
neremba – bird
ngala – no, none
nganya goork – girl
nganyaki, nanyaki – small
nubiyt – water
nyurra wurryn – hullo, welcome
pootpooteyt (KW) – blue wren
punyip – bunyip (literally shark)
teetayarr (KW) – tree creeper
tolom – fish
tolum – duck
toweel (KW) – cousin
wallert (wombeetch) – possum
wanung – brother
warrawan – sore
warre-a – sea
warre-a korraiyn – salty water
wate – to run

weing (wiyn) – fire
wernen – roll
wirran – black cockatoo, yellow tailed
woori garl – dog
wurrung – hut
yani-yu – go away
yellpillup – willy wagtail
yern – moon
yingally – singing
yolla – short-tailed shearwater, mutton bird, moon bird
youdorro – warm
yournit – small fish
yueh (ye ye) – yes

Wathaurong is a sister language to the Bunurong language. The two share close language association, boundaries, customs, ceremony and fate.

KW denotes words from the Kirrae wurrong language

Also from Bruce Sims Books

Zeno's Paradise
A novel by Bron Nicholls

Cornucopia City is divided against itself.

North of the river, the estuary is being poisoned and homeless children barely survive in deserted warehouses.

South of the river, the suburbs are green and pleasant. Martha Wellwright, radio talkshow host, lives with her family on the edge of a beautiful park. Zeno the Head Gardener has made a haven of order and tranquillity, where Martha's twin children are safe.

But nothing is as cleanly divided, or as safe, as it appears to be. The politics and economics of the late twentieth century catch up with Zeno's park, and the familiar routines of many people are disturbed: Pastor Ronny Hatchell, evangelist and developer; Maria and Vicente, illegal immigrants; Titania, director of the Midsummer Night's Dream company; half-mad Mervyn, inventor of *Realspace computer games. All, along with Martha's family and Zeno, find themselves staring into the heart of the Knowledge of Good and Evil.

Zeno's Paradise is a collision of many myths, old and new, which remind us how little we've changed when we are up against greed, jealousy and the desire for revenge; and love, of course.

Also from Bruce Sims Books

Heddy and Me
Susan Varga

'I notice, and not for the first time, that Mother glows when she talks of the war years, whereas her face fades and strains when we get to the present. Back then, the stage was large, and irrational forces dictated events. Now the wars are subtle and small and there never is a clear victory. Fighting your loved ones over well-worn territory. Fighting, in a way, over the outcome of those big years.'

Heddy and Me spans the twentieth century and some of its greatest upheavals: war, the holocaust, immigration.

In telling her mother's story, Susan Varga also tells her own. As a tiny baby she barely survived the holocaust, in hiding in a Hungarian village with her sister and her mother, Heddy. Neither the pain nor the devastation of this time lessened Heddy's will to go on and to recreate her life in Australia.

'... a seamless narrative. Varga's story of her mother and grandmother's life before and during the Nazi era is written with a classic simplicity and effortless flow ...' Mary Rose Liverani, *The Australian*

'This is a challenging, complex, rich, and above all, humane book. Into the process of creating it has gone great frankness and courage, and a hard-won recognition of the potential for destructiveness in the closest, most loving relationships.' Sara Dowse, *Canberra Times*

Flight 642: Jakarta to Dili
An Australian journal
Jane Nicholls

In Jakarta, Jane Nicholls and her co-workers had to decide whether to flee or stay put in the terrifying breakdown of the rule of law before the repressive Soeharto regime fell.

Over a year later, living in a house that served as the office of the Fretilin Central Committee, she was admitted to the remarkable family of East Timorese, a people who were daring to hope that their freedom would come at last.

'Tonight we women talk about how it will be when the result of the ballot is known and the people have won. ''I will dance in the streets, and cry until I have no crying left.'' ''But Jane,'' says another, suddenly intensely serious, ''after the result of the ballot is known, and whether we win or lose, there will be a terrible massacre. Worse than 1975. We know that for certain and we are prepared.'' '

In her journal, Nicholls reflects on some of the complexities of Indonesia and East Timor. The actions of the military and the economic crisis are seen in human terms at ground level – the lives of people caught up in momentous national events, living in truly dangerous times. Its stage is the kitchen and the office as well as the streets of destruction and death.

It is the story of the everyday of history.

Bruce Sims Books are distributed by:

Australian Book Group

The distribution centre is care of Landmark Warehouse
PO Box 130, Drouin, Victoria 3818

Phone: 03 5625 4290

FAX: 03 5625 3756

Bookshops should enquire at these numbers to order or for
the contact details of their nearest sales representative.

Individual or bulk orders please contact the publisher.